Rakesh Kumar (R.K.) Sing
Reserve Police Force (CRPF)
fiction and non-fiction – rang _____ ...ologies
to Naxalism, as well as novels. ...ritten more than
100 articles in leading newspap... and magazines on diverse
subjects such as management and behavioural science.

In his 25 years of service in CRPF, he has been decorated with
several medals from the Government and ten Commendation
Discs. He has served in conflict zones such as Kashmir and
in the north-east besides in areas like Dantewada in Bastar in
Chhattisgarh, affected by Naxalism. He is a resource person in
the Bureau of Police Research and Development and delivers
lectures at various police academies.

He has received the prestigious Govind Ballav Pant
Purashkar for his books – *Naxalwaad aur Police ki Bhumikaa* in
2011 and *Naxalwaad – Ankaha Sacch* in 2021. While commanding
his unit in Bastar in 2019, his unit was adjudged as the Best
Operational Battalion.

He can be reached on his e-mail at rksingh47@gmail.
com; on Twitter at @rksingh4971. *Lockdown Love* is the author's
second novel in English, the first one being, *Colours of Red*.

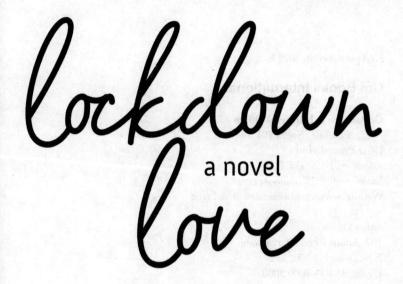

lockdown love

a novel

Rakesh Kumar Singh

Om Books International

First published in 2022 by

Om Books International

Corporate & Editorial Office
A-12, Sector 64, Noida 201 301
Uttar Pradesh, India
Phone: +91 120 477 4100
Email: editorial@ombooks.com
Website: www.ombooksinternational.com

Sales Office
107, Ansari Road, Darya Ganj,
New Delhi 110 002, India
Phone: +91 11 4000 9000
Fax: +91 11 2327 8091
Email: sales@ombooks.com
Website: www.ombooks.com

ISBN: 978-93-91258-94-8

Printed in India

10 9 8 7 6 5 4 3 2 1

1

7th May, 2020
44th day of lockdown

"I don't want to die, Vikram," Nisha's voice sounded weak and brittle. She was lying on a wooden double bed in a government transit officers' hostel; hiding from the police and the administration.

She was lying there, waiting to die.

Her transformation from a beautiful, intelligent, charming and warm young woman to a near corpse with a wan pallor, barely breathing, had taken just a few days. The beauty and the fragrance of the wild red roses and lavender passion flowers on the table next to her bed were not enough to lift the mire that was slowly drawing her into its murky depths.

Her condition was more agonising than the pain of the bullet that had pierced Vikram's body ten years ago. Tears pricked his eyes, softening the contours of his strong face and filling his heart with grief – and a new compassion. Nisha had tested positive for the Coronavirus and was withering in the isolation ward of New Delhi's Safdarjung Hospital, where she had worked as a doctor for the last thirteen years. She had no one to help her tide over the crisis, and she would have rather preferred to die than suffer alone, quarantined in the hospital.

Disillusionment and despair were rife in the country, rather across the world. But it was far gloomier in the 'Corona' wards of the hospitals where the tally of the dead had surged in the last few days. The body count was taking a toll on both the patients and caregivers' mental health. The pressure of the increasing number of patients to be treated and tended, to in post Covid care was impacting the health of the care-workers. They were picking up the virus from the Corona positive patients. The doctors were fast becoming the new infantry in the fight against the virus — and also the new tribe of martyrs.

Dr. Nisha Garg, struggling to cope with the loneliness and the frustration of the hospital that reeked of decay and death, agreed to Colonel Vikram Rathore's suggestion to escape from the isolation ward to spend what she thought were her last days with Vikram. He had promised her a 'love heaven', hidden from the world. She thought that even if she had to die, it would be a death worthwhile. She had never been touched with affection, or ever eyed with longing.

Vikram had fled from his unit, which he commanded, to be with her. He had been seeking a deeper meaning in life. Although he had a successful career as a 'sentinel of the nation', he realised that his life was void of inner joy and contentment. Of late, he was having difficulty in sleeping and a sense of guilt stalked him round-the-clock like a beast of prey.

He felt that he had been unjust and 'immoral' in his pursuit of a self-centered style of life. He repented for the wrongs he had committed. This compelled him to take the extreme and unexpected step of deserting the unit. He did so after being denied leave because of the continuous skirmishes with infiltrators from across the border with neighbouring Pakistan at his unit's forward posts. A *fidayeen* – terrorist – attack at the unit headquarters just two days ago had killed two soldiers and injured a lieutenant colonel.

Now both of them were fugitives, having broken probably a thousand rules in the last few days. The police were hunting for them. Especially, as their motive for running away was unknown. The road ahead seemed rough but they were not devastated, for they refused to dwell on the consequences of their action. They were living for the moment.

Who could ever imagine that a *Shaurya Chakra* – bravery medal – winner, a Colonel in the Indian Army, and a successful senior doctor of one of the most prestigious hospitals in the country would run away, in the hope that love and care would cure the disease, not the isolation and the life-supporting gadgets of the Corona wards, bleak in their clinical prognosis of the fates trapped within the confines.

It was sheer insanity, at least on the part of a senior doctor who had been dealing with the 'Corona cases', to think with her heart and the wild rush of emotions. Isolation wards and quarantining patients' first contacts were Nisha's ideas. A formidable talent in the medical fraternity, she had been at the forefront with the leading doctors of government hospitals, in plotting strategies to battle the virus. She was a core member of the team of experts who were drafting Corona-related instructions, which the government issued from time-to-time.

The decision to run away was not a freak or a juvenile one. It was driven by a passion and commitment to preserve what had been left out in life. They were in love with life again.

Eliminating the unpleasant side of the escapade, Vikram turned his thoughts to the philosophy of life and the very purpose of it. It had been the best excuse to justify anything one wanted to do.

"Who is going to die? We haven't come here to die but to live and love. We should live each moment in joy and not in the fear of death."

Vikram lay beside Nisha, holding her hand, reassuring her that 'all is well'. Cheering and comforting came naturally to him. Though both were physically weak, they still felt the healing warmth of their interlocked palms, auguring hope to begin from where they had left off many years ago.

Nisha faltered, a faint smile played on her lips. "True, I should not be greedy now. I eloped with you in my old age to live in the moment and not to hanker for the months and the years, which you have denied me for the last thirteen years." They had finally understood the absurdities of life without love.

"Aha! Is it only me? Good! A woman will never stop complaining. Okay then, I am not going to share my tea with you." Vikram pretended to be angry and turned around to the other side, holding the mug of tea from which both were to sip — and slurp on the trifling joys of life. It was an old childhood ritual. Nisha mustered strength, ascended on her pillow and holding Vikram from behind, rested her head on his back. "You are my cup of tea. I will have you, dear," she said softly.

Tears misted Vikram's eyes. He dared not look at her. He knew Nisha might not survive the illness. Why he had wasted his life away from her for so many years. He wiped the tears from his eyes, turned around and hugged her.

The nearness gave them strength. After sometime, he broke the embrace, saying, "Let me make tea again."

"Oh shit! I thought I chose a hot boyfriend. My bad luck." She jested, trying to rile Vikram into reacting. Vikram had a reputation with women and they both burst into laughter.

Sipping tea together in beds, balconies and lawns had been part of their school day dreams – teenage fantasies. Even after so many years, the dream was still as fresh as ever. Vikram refilled the cup and brought it to her. Exchange or rather 'sharing' was crucial to the ritual. First, they sipped the tea from their respective cups and then exchanged the cups to drink the brew, 'touched' by the other. They believed that the little 'ceremony' made their tea tastier and their love deeper.

It was their fifteenth day in hiding. Vikram sat up for prayers on his bed, and with folded hands wished that the Corona warriors would defeat the virus and the world to go back to loving and hugging each other soon. He told Nisha that it was *Buddha Purnima* – the full moon of Buddha's birth – that day, and they must celebrate it. He asked her to dress for a dance in the evening as the moon was pink. The Colonel was not a dancer but he knew Nisha loved to dance. She often said that dance was a form of meditation to heal stress and cure sadness. The offer brought a broad smile to her face as she thought about the music and the steps she would choose for the evening.

Vikram went into the kitchen, thinking what he would cook for dinner. He was always indecisive in the kitchen. Nisha wondered how he made decisions in a fraction of a second in combat situations. Vikram brought out a few 'ready-to-eat' food packets from the kitchen cabinet and after long deliberations with his own dissipated self – or perhaps his alter ego – he sought Nisha's consent. Food had to be *prêt* for the night.

He opened a packet of instant *biriyani* – rice with spice – and cooked it. Heaping the steaming *biriyani* with tomato ketchup on a platter, he fed Nisha with a spoon. He cuddled her like a baby and massaged her head so that she could sleep well. She needed rest. She had turned pale of late and even the minor chores of routine personal care tired her.

Though his immunity and strength were better than hers, he, too, was fatigued. But the battle against Corona called for strict hygiene. He dusted the apartment in the morning, wiping the grime off the corners, and filled the drinking water bottles, a jar and then a big tub. The running water supply was limited to fixed hours in this house. Cleaning utensils and the rooms were new to him. Nonetheless, it was now part of his journey from darkness to light, acts of cleansing. Life had taken so many twists and turns during this short period of a month-and-a-half. He had come to her from Drass, the frozen mountains up north, embraced the Coronavirus and both of them were ready to die if life denied them another chance. A second chance at this point seemed remote because of their worsening condition. They were on a path of uncertainties to explore new possibilities. It presented a curious canvas of contrasts to Vikram, used to slim chances in life as an armyman.

Nisha's words, "I don't want to die, Vikram", haunted him. Anxiety made him tense, heartbroken and always near to tears – *the break point*, he mused to himself. He leapt out of the bed and went to the balcony to hide his turmoil from her. He was her only strength and he didn't want to disillusion her. They didn't want to die before fulfilling their fondest wish in life, being together, but the Coronavirus was in no mood to make way for them to bend the barricades. He appeared lost. The train of thoughts sometime made him absent-minded.

Just then, he heard Nisha scream...

2

22nd March, 2020
Janta Curfew day

Was this the beginning of the end or was it a new beginning?

The narrative had begun to take shape in the last few days. Colonel Vikram Rathore's life started changing suddenly. Exactly from Sunday, 22nd March, 2020. The weather was cold but not as icy as it was usually in Drass in March. There had been sporadic rain in the last five-six days but no snowfall, which kept the temperature moderate. The Himalayas were beautiful in March, covered in a white robe of snow. The rays of the sun touched the pristine mountain caps, sparkling off the ice, making them seemingly diamond encrusted and dazzling. They almost kissed the sky.

The cool breeze gently touching his face was like a union with heaven. Sitting on the lawn and staring at the sky, Vikram felt close to the endless blue of it. This vast swathe of blue held so much of hope and dreams for everyone. The brightness of the morning seemed to put his mind at rest. Left to loneliness, the Coronavirus was not the only mystery he wanted to decode today. With a mug of freshly-brewed coffee in his hand, he walked towards the end of the lawn fronting his bungalow at the edge of an elevated patch of land, on which the residence of the commanding officer was located. Below him, Vikram could see his unit – 19/5 Rajput Rifles – spread over acres to the left and beyond that, the deep gorge. The soldiers of the legendary unit were busy in their routine activities, oblivious to their commanding officer's worries. He was thinking how difficult it was for him to be playful and jovial like his troops. He saw his troops saluting the flag of the regiment proudly while passing by it. He saw the monogram of his regiment embossed on the mug from which he was sipping coffee. He felt elated that he was commanding a battalion of this legendary regiment.

The Prime Minister had issued a call for *Janta Curfew* that day to check the spread of Corona. It was to be observed voluntarily by people from 7 a.m. to 9 p.m. The aim of the curfew, as the government claimed, was to make the people understand the concept of social distancing and the need to stay at home. The Coronavirus had triggered a crisis worldwide. Everyone was clueless about what to do. Social distancing was the only measure that had proven to be effective against the virus so far. Every government was pursuing its citizens to follow it, failing which, they were imposing 'lockdowns'. Experts were saying that India should have enforced the 'lockdown' sooner; for once the virus invaded the country in full force, it would be difficult to leash the spread.

Being a Sunday, it helped. Everyone was at home. But the stay was kind of imposed. There were some disgruntled voices. But most people followed it diligently. The Prime Minister had also requested people to ring bells or beat plates at 1700 hrs in support of the doctors, nurses and other frontline workers, who were fighting the pandemic.

The *Janta Curfew* provided everyone time to think and reflect. For some, it was a once-in-a-lifetime experience to witness a global pandemic up close, while for others, it was a source of distress. Life showed up in quixotic *avatars* — beckoning, coaxing, giving and taking away.

The virus gave Vikram time to reminisce about his relationship with Nisha.

They had met 26 years ago in the activity hall of the Modern School in New Delhi. They were both in Patel House but in different sections. She was in Class 9. Nisha Garg was a pretty and bubbly girl and Vikram Rathore was a naughty and handsome boy. She was good in academics, whereas he was an avid sportsman, a movie buff. Sharp and witty, Vikram was an excellent debater and participated in various debating competitions at public forums. Unsurprisingly, they met in the run-up to a debate. He was unexpectedly asked to represent the school in a debate on 'Political Uncertainties in the Middle-East Countries are a Creation of Vested Interests of Western Powers', of which he had no background knowledge. She came to his rescue. She had a good knowledge of contemporary incidents happening around the world – of current affairs. She told Vikram that she read the newspapers daily and also went through two to three magazines, every month. Her eyes shone, eager to share her knowledge. Vikram made notes from her detailed briefing and firmed up his talking points. He did very well that day in the debate. Nisha was happy because he gave her full credit of it in front of everyone. Her pride was evident.

Thereafter, they started speaking to each other more often, mostly about current affairs. And, gradually about other things like movies, common friends and career choices. Whenever Vikram didn't want to read up on a subject, he would ask Nisha to read instead and brief him. In a few months, their classmates left the duo to themselves.

They didn't know exactly when they started liking each other, and then loving. Like any teenage romance, their love was dreamy – full of fantasies and aspirations to a shared future.

Nisha's parents were professors and the family's focus had always been on academics. They had two daughters and a son. Both the girls wanted to be doctors, and the son, an IT engineer or a technocrat, so that he could migrate to USA, Canada or Australia. Everyone in her family was always in a learning mode, trying to move up the ladder. It impressed Vikram. He started updating his knowledge – and brush his intellect – to impress her.

Vikram's father was an executive officer in the Delhi government and his mother was a home-maker. Vikram was their eldest son. Their younger son, Anurag, was more sincere about his studies and knew what he wanted to do in life. He was not confused about his career choices like Vikram, and nor was he as creative as Vikram. In time, both grew up and worked hard at fulfilling their ambitions. Anurag was now settled in his profession. Nisha's brother Ashu migrated to America, and her sister Sonu to Canada.

When they were in high school, their proximity and interest in each other raised eyebrows of many of their common friends. That Vikram and Nisha were in love was known to their siblings, but their parents were clueless. Their families bonded at the parent-teacher meetings in school, as a social group.

However, for the last thirteen years, Vikram and Nisha had not spoken to each other. Their love was lost somewhere in the maze of their disparate trajectories in life.

The epidemic was testing time for health workers. The life of the doctors had become too stressful. They were working in seclusion and were not permitted to interact with common people, sometimes even their patients. The Safdarjung Hospital, where Nisha worked, was next to the All India Institute of

Medical Sciences in the busy southern reaches of Delhi. The hospital had devised a new method to keep doctors in touch with people, other than the Corona patients. They were put on rotation to attend to the hospital helpline number. It was a kind of stress-buster that was being tried out. The infection was sudden, and health workers across the world were still exploring the best methods to fight it. The situation was quite alarming. The doctors and nurses, as the first responders, were suffering a lot, mentally as well as in terms of loss of life. All over the world, people and the governments had begun to call them the 'Corona Warriors.'

Vikram's life had started taking an unusual turn since 26th January, the day he received the *Shaurya Chakra* from the President, an award for exemplary act of bravery. It was not the first time his bravery was recognised, but this was the highest medal of honour he had ever received. The whole country saw it on the Republic day broadcast on television. Admiration and praise flowed for the next few days. But in a corner of his 'gallant heart' upon which he had always prided himself, Vikram felt forlorn. At times, he hated himself. He was filled with remorse for many things he had done. There were so many wrongs he had committed, but those 'offenses' did not matter to the people, who were glorifying him now. Or maybe, those were minor administrative mistakes and operational excesses. In his personal life, things were not easy to understand. The right and the wrongs blurred into smoky lines.

Therefore, what he had done to Nisha was not something which sat well with him, now. He was keen to understand himself. He was exploring everything – sometimes randomly, sometimes what his friends advised him. He was impatient during the day, anxious and sleepless at night. He had lost his appetite, and his zeal to remain fit physically had vanished, too. He stopped going to the gym and playing badminton or tennis. He confined himself at home after work. The glory of the heroic acts of the battalion that he was commanding no longer ignited his feelings, sparking enthusiasm and energy. An intense absorption of solitude was slowly sapping his life lines. It was like he was being smuggled into solitary confinement.

On the Prime Minister's call to beat *thalis* – platters – or ring bells as a mark of respect and gratitude to Corona care-givers, he responded with the whole battalion at 1700 hrs. He ensured that someone had taken a few photographs, too. Nisha should see them. The endorsement – beating of *thalis* – was not only an expression of his gratitude to her profession, but also his personal appreciation for her. The hills reverberated with the sound of bells and *thalis* being beaten by the soldiers. He stood on the balcony ringing the yellow metal bell he had hung in his home temple. Diligently, and very lovingly.

The thought that haunted him was, *Why he had acted that way with Nisha?*

3

23rd March, 2020
Monday

A Google search provided him abundance of information – the world was going through a depressing time. China was in the grip of new virus known as Corona, later renamed COVID-19. It had originated in Wuhan, in Hubei province. The virus spread by contact with an infected person or from places contaminated by those infected – by sneezing, coughing and touching. Or even breathing, some said. There was no cure so far and the only possible prevention was keeping away from those who were infected. If you maintained a distance of two metres, you were probably armed with a Covid shield. To control the spread of the virus, the term 'social distancing' had become popular; urging people to keep a measure of distance between themselves. It was disgusting. It was advised that handshakes, hugging or even touching a person, in any way, should be avoided. Even if one was not infected. People were practicing a new kind of untouchability. The first case was detected on 8 December, 2019, but the disease was labeled as a pandemic from the first week of January. People were advised to stay at home or were being locked in their residences in Wuhan. The death rates were very high in China.

The first case was reported in India on 31 January, as in the US. Around the world, the situation was so bad that in certain countries, armies were being called in to handle law and order issues.

Vikram was jittery. His immediate worry was to protect his own troops from this pandemic and then make the soldiers available to the government to utilise their services to fight this virus. Social distancing was another cause of concern for the troops. Troops worked in teams. Their motivation came by the way of high fives and hugs. Even in the worst of the time, an encouraging pat on the back or a handshake changed the mood. But now, there was social distancing. A minimum distance of two metres had to be maintained. First of all, it was highly demotivating. Secondly, in barracks and on duty, such distances were difficult to keep. Barracks were cramped. It had never been the priority of any government to make life easy for the soldiers. Barracks were not designed to provide social distancing—hence deemed unsafe by many inside.

But the soldier could not battle alone. Social distancing was a threat to the organisational fabric of the army. The situation was novel, unimagined. 'Stay home and stay safe' had become the new *mantra* in life. Like any law-abiding officer, Vikram's primary duty was to enforce these guidelines. Reports from all over the world indicated that for law enforcement agencies, it was an arduous task to get the 'lockdowns' enforced. Armymen were attacked, Corona positive persons spat on them and hated them for forcing them to stay indoors — depressed and often starving. There were also people, who were hiding their illness and venturing out, jeopardising the lives of others.

Vikram called a meeting of his officers and an 'order group' of the battalion to plan strategies to fight the challenge. He passed the message that the army headquarters and the government had circulated. They wanted to maintain strict discipline despite the challenges posed in fighting the virus, but all of them needed to learn and cope. The first need was not to get infected.

In the army, a junior never disobeys commands issued by seniors. Once the colonel ordered safety-checks, everyone obeyed.

"Sir, it will be done."

He knew the brief. It was not just winning the battle, he had to care for the lives in question. Sacrificing life for a cause was a done thing in the army. But this was not an assignment that called for chivalry or bravery, it required 'social distancing'. The weapon was the challenge. He could well imagine the confusion the order caused when he announced it to his battalion, even though they echoed compliance. He then asked everyone for suggestions about how to execute this task.

The biggest issue was living in the cramped barracks. It was decided to put more persons on duty for some kind of patrolling or skill-enhancing battle exercises to avoid crowded quarters. The timings in the dining area were divided and spread through the day. Cooks and *safai karamcharis* – cleaners – had to be provided masks and gloves. Contacts with people outside was minimised. But he was not sure how to handle the troops, who would be at risk, while assisting civilians and infected people.

The Quarter Master of the unit was instructed to ensure that basic stores were available and whatever was not, was to be procured immediately from the brigade headquarters. The biggest challenge was to source the most necessary protective gear against the virus. These items were not easily available as hoarders had depleted supplies. Greed made him angry; he could not figure out why people were so greedy even in times of crisis.

Vikram summoned a '*Sainik Sammelan*' – a soldiers' forum – to formally address the troops. He spoke to them with sympathy and concern about the forthcoming dangers that the pandemic could throw up. The troops were genuinely worried about their families and their personal safety – and it was of paramount importance to make them aware of the Corona hazards. He told them to educate their families immediately about the pandemic.

He was clear in his message – the World Health Organization and China had failed to contain the virus. They needed to remember that plans never failed, individuals failed. But the soldiers were firm in their faith. It is the Indian Army, it doesn't fail ever. And his own battalion, NEVER EVER at all.

For a change, he was satisfied that his utility was still felt by his troops. He was happy today.

Happiness brings magic to life.

The schedule was hectic till lunch for Vikram. There were instructions from the government to gear up to face the problems and come forward to help the common man. The mission would bring plenty of confusion and anxiety in course, which had to be dealt with delicately. He called a meeting of his officers and briefed them about their tasks. A new reporting format was circulated, which had added a column about the virus. 'Dos' and 'don'ts' were to be made available to all the soldiers and a medical team was kept on alert to help soldiers as well as citizens.

After lunch, he retired to his room. He had no intention of going to work in the evening, or to attend anything official unless there was a crisis. Lying on the bed, he felt proud of himself like a boy that how important he still was to his unit. But then, his mood suddenly turned sombre. Nisha interrupted his thoughts. He could not forget her. He began to think about her, their lives till a few years back and what went wrong.

One of the most decorated officers in the Indian Army, Colonel Vikram Rathore had achieved heroic successes while commanding his battalion in the war zones of the Northern Corps and in the most controversial conflict theatre of Kashmir with his brilliant battle tactics. He had completed seventeen years of service in the Army and was now 40-years-old. Not quite old enough to be so disenchanted with the glory and glamour of the forces, but he was moody and kind-hearted. The troops under his command felt his innate compassion many times, like when he stopped them from being harsh even with the terrorists. He always handled women and elderly people with gentle kindness. He shouted at his subordinates for not working sincerely, but strangely, he tolerated genuine mistakes. Slips and lags irritated Vikram. He was a true friend of the soldiers, he commanded.

However, these days he was mostly silent.

He was also wondering why Noor had called him last week, after ages. She must have made a lot of effort to get his contact number of the unit. He was away visiting a post, so he could not receive the call. She was the same woman, who 15 years ago as a teenager, had alleged that he had raped her. So, why did she want to get in touch with him now. He was curious about the call.

Another surprise was a series of messages which could be termed as flirtatious from General Mittal's daughter Pankhuri on WhatsApp. Vikram had recently received a painting from her as well, and other forwarded messages. He was not sure how to react to her overtures. She was married to a powerful officer in the civil services. But 'happily married' is such a misnomer. She had her own aspirations and was quite enterprising, too. The general wanted Vikram to marry Pankhuri. She was an amazing girl. Intelligent, sensuous and glamorous, she had mesmerised Vikram. He had warmed up to the idea of marrying her — it had eased the shadows of gloom that often hung heavy over him.

Then life suddenly took a strange twist and their romance fizzled out. The general had not forgotten or forgiven Vikram. He had promised that one day he would take the 'shit out of Vikram'. However, this was long ago. Pankhuri now had a well-placed husband. Happily-married Pankhuri was probably flirting to beat the boredom of social distancing or wanted some extra fun; he was not sure.

Vikram wondered whether he should contact all of them, even the General. It could lead him to a complex maze, but take care of his loneliness. Or, maybe, they were in distress and needed him. He couldn't care. It was best to keep these chapters closed. Generally, when he felt sad or lonely, he preferred to light a cigar or drink a cup of strong black coffee and move to the lawn or lock himself in his bedroom. In those moments, he did not forget to pick out a book from the shelf to read or a fountain pen to write; though these days, he rarely managed to do either. However, his passion was not dead. He still thought that his intellectual ability was better than his battle efficiency and he could write poetry better than he planned an operational strategy. He had been at the forefront of low-intensity border conflicts for years now.

Thinking about the conflict made him analytical — also introspective. Cross-border terrorism could gain ground only after brainwashing some vulnerable sections of the population, the Colonel believed. The Kashmir valley had been a fertile breeding ground, especially for religious fundamentalism. Religious fundamentalism has been the single largest murderer in the world, aided and abetted by cross-border terrorism. The Colonel had observed this on a day-to-day basis, while posting vigil on the border.

He had seen young people dying. When children around the world were scaling new highs, these orthodox border inhabitants under threat from religious fanatics, were making their children sit in prayer for hours, indoctrinating them with hatred.

They even spurned progressive government schemes in the name of religion. They believed that life was much better after death, if courted in the name of god. Being in the army, he knew that death did not sound that bad. If it was for the right cause.

A soldier was trained to take pride in death as supreme sacrifice. It was an honour to die for the country and return home wrapped in the national colours. That was the code of life and death in the armed forces. War had always been important. Centuries ago, it was the question of survival, then it turned into a manic greed to grab new lands or plunder new wealth. Now, war was an ego-kick for leaders at the political helm or for a bunch of people, who wanted their nations to become superpowers.

Such profundities kept the colonial occupied. Of late, the Colonel had stopped going out to meet friends or fellows. Consequently, they had also stopped coming to him. Once people are able to make out that you are not receptive to them, they fade away.

Friendships and associations needed warmth to flourish. The Colonel was jovial by nature and naturally drew a wide circle of friends. But then, he realised that they were just mundane company to while away with, in leisure. He probably needed a different kind of companionship — a bonding that should make him realise life's truths or the depths of love. He wanted to express his unspoken feelings to someone. The heart craved for a free rein, an unbridled run. An escape from the clutches of high moral values to the world of attachment with a person on Ground Zero — someone, who echoed on the same wavelength.

Some of his colleagues were not surprised at his behavioural change. He often swung between highs and lows during his early years in the army. He would think differently from others, which very few were able to digest. Nevertheless, Vikram was a wonderful friend; always standing by mates and cracking jokes even in the most stressful situations. He shared his time and resources freely without bitterness. He preferred to be in good company, often picking up dinner tabs at clubs and restaurants. But the Corona was changing the way he lived. Vikram avoided personal contacts with everyone.

His life's philosophy was also transforming.

4

24th March, 2020

PM's address to the nation at 8 pm

Vikram felt restive. He diverted his restlessness by immersing himself at work in the office and calling his colleagues. He called his friends, many of whom were surprised because he was calling them after months. Then, he called his father. His parents were alone these days as his younger brother was abroad.

"Papa, hope you and Ma are doing fine. Ma's health is being taken care of?" he asked. A twinge of guilt haunted him.

"Yes, we are fine. But your mother is not happy with you. You have not visited us for the last four months."

"Yes papa, I know but you are aware it has been a grueling time for us in the last six months. Many things were happening after the scrapping of Article 370 and we were always on high alert."

"Whatever it is, your mother does not understand it. And she is right, too. Come soon," his father was emphatic. Parents seek the company of their children as they age. They want someone to talk to, eat with – someone to take care of them.

His father Anup Singh Rathore, a retired government servant, had been a principled man throughout his life. The only thing which he earned was respect. By the grace of god, both his sons had sustained and took care of him and his wife. Anurag, the Colonel's younger brother, was based in Bangalore. He was excelling in his profession, and travelled outside the country often. All was well, apparently. But the Colonel's mother was always worried. She did not like the fact that Vikram was in the army – or that he had not married yet.

"Why do you need to take so much risk in life? Do we not have enough money or land? Then, why this perilous army job?" She cribbed every time she spoke to him.

She always thought that Vikram's life was weird. He had been different from the beginning. His behaviour was difficult to understand. He did not tread a simple path. He sat for the National Defence Academy's entrance test after completing high school; qualified for it, but just a day before reporting for training, he decided that it was not the right time for him to join the army. He had to explore the world. His mother was happy with the decision. But his father was skeptical.

"Why let go of such a good opportunity to be in a job which gives financial stability and respect in the society?"

Vikram graduated with a degree in Creative Arts from Delhi University. During his years in college, he wrote poetry and short stories. An emotional person, he believed that art was the true emotional partner. A man can express his emotions in various forms of art. He had explored different genres of art. He was not yet sure about his career. But when he was in college, Pakistan had violated India's borders and it soon escalated into a war-like scenario, which culminated into the Kargil War in 1999.

Indian troops had discovered the Kargil aggression quite late, making it more deadly for the Indian Army to take on the enemy. Many young officers and soldiers died. The troops were caught unaware because it was a war fought after decades of lull. Who goes to war these days? No one can be victorious. A winning country is also a loser because wars are such costly propositions, putting the people at risk of penury and pain.

Apologetically explaining himself, Vikram said "Papa, you know that I was about to come, but then the protests started and now Corona is causing panic, I have to stay back." Nevertheless, he understood that like any other busy young man, who forgets to take care of old folks at home, he had erred, too. It was preposterous. Why was he so busy? Whatever the circumstances may have been, he could have spared time to speak to them. But he had not done so in the last few weeks.

It did not strike Vikram that his parents were uncomfortable by themselves. Now, the country was under a 'lockdown'.

"Papa, why don't you come to me here in my camp. Things will be managed much better and you will not face any difficulty." He lied, but his concern was genuine. He had not called to invite them. He did not know where he had been lost all these days? If he couldn't go, why he had not called his parents to join him?

Vikram realised that he was completely out of sync for the last two months.

Surprising, as he was generally a balanced person. His parents must have been worried about him. They were not too inquisitive about his moods. Everyone was aware of his dedication to the cause, which he considered good for people. Simultaneously, it was also known among his family and close coteries that he was determined to follow his ambitions. It had always been hard to make him yield to pressure.

After graduating, he became a freelance travel and content writer. But the Kargil war had stirred him; set him thinking. He appeared for the Combined Defense Services examination and qualified easily.

***

The Prime Minister had tweeted that the he would address the nation at 8 pm Last time, when he addressed the country on 8th November at 8 pm in 2016, he announced demonetisation of 1,000 and 500 rupee notes. That was popularly known as *Notebandi* – scrapping of currency. It was widely expected that a *deshbandi*, a 'lockdown' would be announced to enforce social distancing. It would be a new experience for the country. There was much speculation about the kind of restrictions that could be imposed. There was panic buying among people who could afford it. Nobody knew the possible extent of the 'lockdown'. Very soon, domestic flights were likely to be shut down, too. Medicines and ration were being stocked. Suddenly everyone was talking about the Coronavirus and the audacity of China in suppressing information about it. Some believed it was a biological weapon developed by China, which had gone wrong.

For some time, since October 2019, the world had been seeing the total 'lockdown' in Wuhan.

5

8 pm, The Hour
PM speaks to the nation

As expected, the Prime Minister announced a complete 'lockdown' from midnight for three weeks to control the spread of the pandemic.

It was expected that some drastic measures would be taken like *deshbandi*. Two days ago, he had asked for a self-imposed curfew and named it *Janta Curfew* – which was a huge success. But the severity of the pandemic was such that it was not only spreading exponentially across the world, but killing hundreds too. The death toll in the first flush of the Corona had gone up to 20,000 across the world and more than 300,000 were infected.

In India, the number of cases was still low, around 500. If it exploded, the country would be unable to manage the spread; alarm bells were ringing in the government corridors. Countries with the best healthcare systems in the world had almost collapsed due to the enormity of the infection. India, with a population of 1,300 million, mostly in crowded cities and big villages, was a tinder keg for a virus disaster. Utmost precaution was needed, more so, because people did not understand the gravity of the situation nor they were equipped with resources at their disposal to remain in isolation, and sustain.

All forms of public transport had been pulled off the road. The 'lockdown' was for three weeks, up to 14th April. Only essential services were to be kept open under strict monitoring. It was a sort of country-wide curfew to stop the community spreading stage of the pandemic, or the third stage.

This move was generally welcomed. Survival was the first priority. People do not adhere to advisories and warnings, easily; they have to be forced into it. They need coercive intervention. Everyone thinks he is on the right path and no harm can come to them or their families. They were insulated from the virus. Such perceptions had already caused much damage.

The late reaction of the Chinese government in declaring the true nature of the virus had destroyed and stigmatised Wuhan. It was in all probability a man-made disaster. It was being widely believed that China had delayed informing the world about the severity of the virus by more than one or two weeks. Wuhan was a commercial city trading with many countries for centuries. Businessmen had travelled in January and February to and from Wuhan, thus spreading the virus, globally, it was cited. The chain kept enlarging in progression till many countries across several continents were forced to lock down.

No one was sure about the right way to stop the spread of the virus. The only precaution was social distancing to break the infection chain. The government was exploring every possible measure to protect the people. Medical experts had divergent views about the disease, but all were unanimous about the need for 'social distancing'. Even people in the remote villages were following it strictly, stopping the entry of outsiders into their villages by putting up barricades of logs and trees – makeshift bamboo fences – at entry points.

This also showed that when it was a question of life, people adapted to survival strategies quickly. When the virus first surfaced in China, no country could believe that the strain could unleash such a carnage. Thousands had died within weeks.

The 'lockdown' announcement came us a rude jolt to Vikram. He was surprised that the country would lock down so soon. He thought that the way the virus was spreading in India was well within limits, and under control. 'Lockdown' was a major crisis in a developing country like India with a population of more than a billion. The curfew left millions of poor people, who migrated across the country for work, stranded. It took away their livelihoods.

These poor people would need support of a huge scale. Then, there was resentment that this disease had been brought in by foreign travellers and the 'rich'. After all, there was hardly any hue and cry about diseases of which the poor died. Recently, hundreds of kids and new born babies had died of encephalitis fever, but nobody seemed to be overtly alarmed. Tuberculosis and malnutrition were rampant in the villages.

Human reactions are partial, biased. When someone else has to be stopped, one becomes very conscientious. But when one has to impose it on one's own self, lethargy creeps in. It can be negative ego, as well.

The Colonel was more anguished because his analysis – hypothesis – about how the government would react to the Coronavirus had gone wrong. It bothered him. His strategy and plans had been always right, and he had started thinking that he would be always correct. It was a common syndrome among the army guys. They thought that the country would collapse if angels like them were not around to protect the nation.

Vikram had begun to realise the extent of the challenges ahead of him. The troops would have to be moved for civilian deployment, to tackle people who broke 'lockdown' rules.

They needed to be taken care of with protective gear, masks, nutritious food – and many more things. Medicines and health requirements had to be made available at all times. These resources had to be shared with the common man, too, in this time of calamity and at the same time there was need to keep the troops fighting fit to take on terrorists as well. It was a two-pronged challenge.

As a professional commander, he knew his duty was to take care of the thousand men in his battalion and their families. It was a tough task. But as the saying goes – a commander becomes tougher in tough times. Vikram loved challenges in life. For him, routine was boring. However, what had changed now was his focus on ambitions. He did, what he thought was his duty. Lately, he had lost his determination to excel. He wanted to be the horse, who bore the rider to his destination with diligence; not to be a part of the horse race. In almost two decades of his service, six medals, a dozen appreciations from chiefs and several citations had probably ended his zeal to collect more laurels to adorn his uniform.

It happens in life. But it was too early for Vikram. He had just entered into his forties. Career and life bloom with success in the late 40s and early 50s. He could climb to the top. Who knows one day, he could be the army chief, too? But these did not hold any attraction for him anymore. However, his urge to help those in need had not diminished. Whenever and wherever, he got an opportunity, he rose to the need. He was not dissatisfied with the prospects of his military career but it had lost the allure; nor did he feel a binding loyalty towards the army, now.

For the first time, he thought, *I have had enough of army life.*

He believed he should have quit earlier. The job was killing him.

6

25th March, 2020
1st Day of lockdown

Vikram had been able to convince his parents to come to Drass. Once his parents were there with him, he would be free of worries about them. The pandemic was deadly for the elderly. His parents were in their early seventies. It was a wonderful experience for them to stay in a unit campus, commanded by their son.

The commanding officers' residence was on an elevated patch of land. It was 250 meters off the Srinagar-Leh road, with the mountain ranges to the left. The single-storey spacious house was covered by a blue sheet roof which rippled like an ocean during the day, amidst the surrounding snow. The house had a portico where his official SUV, a Scorpio, stood adorned with the brass metal words 'CO', embossed in a red background on a small rectangular board. The house displayed solemnity and reflected the glory of a proud commander.

The bungalow had seen eminent occupants in the past. Two of them, who had stayed there as commanding officers of their battalions, had become army chiefs.

All the chiefs felt nostalgic about their days as battalion commanders and made it a point to visit their old postings. Past residents would narrate their deeds, or misdeeds and tales of what they did in the house and in the area, when they re-visited old posts. Usually, at length. They didn't bother to check if the present commanding officer was free to listen to their tales. It was a well-established norm that one of the duties of the commanding officers was to listen patiently to the veterans, and even with admiration. When one took over as the commandant of a battalion, the commandant not only expanded his family to bring on board those serving in the unit, but also those who had served there earlier.

That is one of the army's beautiful traditions – wide kinships, bonds inculcating stronger passion and pride.

The threat of Coronavirus was more palpable in the cities. Faraway places like Drass and Kargil, with less movement of people, were considered safer. Travelling to Srinagar by air was not a problem. The airport had been scaled up as an international one. The real beauty of the Valley was its remote hinterlands. Drass was one such place situated between Zoji La pass and Kargil town, known as the gateway to Ladakh. Hardly 140 km from Srinagar city, it was located at a height of 10,800 feet, sprawled on a wide swathe of ice. The temperature dipped to around minus 20-30 degree Celsuis in winter, on an average. A record low in the area was minus 60 degrees.

The bleak weather and the remote location were natural barriers to intrusion by outsiders to Drass. Moreover, restrictions imposed for security reasons warded off the few odd adventurous souls, who wanted to explore the higher Himalayas. This place was strategic to secure the border. In 1948, it fell to attacks and a large chunk of its territory was still under Pakistan's occupation.

The Line of Control has then been a pain for the army.

The population of this area was 1,201 as per the census of 2011. Sometimes, local residents became desperate to meet fellow citizens from the rest of the country.

It was the second coldest region of the world after Siberia. The place was so deserted and cold that during peace-time, the biggest danger was 'white death' from frostbite and freezing. It was the last week of March and the weather was improving. Vikram hoped that the weather would be a lesser threat than the one looming in the form of Covid-19.

This was a strange time for humankind. Never ever had a threat been so widespread across the world. China had reported more than 3,000 deaths and 60,000 infections. But no one believed in China, where free flow of information was restricted. There was widespread understanding that the number of deaths in China was several times more than what it had revealed to the rest of the world. The way Italy and Spain were crushed by the virus was frightening. These countries had failed to ensure precautions at the initial stage and now the body counts were spiraling out of control.

Detailed instructions and protocols were issued by the government and the local agencies. Welfare measures were initiated for the poor, homeless and the daily wage earners. Hospitals were directed to ramp up Covid-special schemes and health checks, suspending all the routine functions, including non-essential surgeries and routine OPD.

People were changing with the scent of death in the air. They were afraid of meeting one another. No one was sure of himself. The fear that stalked everyone was whether they had been infected. If infected, could they detect the infection? If detected, would they recover? Had they infected family members? And finally, would they survive? Life hung on a thin thread.

Despite the almost negligible number of cases in India, so far, one could not ignore the possibility of a proliferation. People took to the lockdown call enthusiastically. They thought that the 'lockdown' would be enough to control the pandemic; it was a kind of auto-defence mechanism of the psyche. Vikram was worried about Nisha's well-being. Being a doctor, she needed to be more active if the situation escalated and that could make her more vulnerable to the infection.

A news flashed on the television screen – domestic flights were terminated from midnight.

He felt that the Coronavirus had further alienated him from Nisha. He tried not to think of her, henceforth.

7

26th March, 2020
2nd Day of Lockdown

"Hi, pigheaded colonel, how are you. Wassup there?

"Hi, Kohli, I am good. And you?"

"I am fine, congratulations. What the fuck did you do? Saw your pic with the minister awarding you a trophy."

"You deserter, rich man! You will not understand. Leave it, how is business – surely you're minting money?"

"Yes, colonel, if I am in business, I have to earn to fund you people for your useless war games."

"Oh! GAMES! Come on, play this game with AK-47s. You will love a bullet in your body?"

Puneet Kohli had called after a long time. Kohli was his batch-mate, but later he left the Army to lead his own life, free from restrictions or calls of duties. He was independent and wanted his own way in life. Even during the days of training, forcing him to do certain things was difficult. But his personality was lovable. He had good insight and astute understanding of unforeseen situations. Therefore, even instructors, who were not happy with his rebellious ways, liked him. He was a happy-go-lucky person, but a master in handling 'impossible' situations.

Kohli always prided himself on being a person of taste. Vikram agreed. Nobody had ever seen him cribbing about anything. Though everything about Kohli's personality was not likable – like his habit of chewing *paan* – betel leaf – and making faces even during normal conversation or his chest-thumping dialogues to justify anything that he thought was important, and had to be defended. He was sometimes too assertive and argumentative but was generally quite affable. He was also a connoisseur of liquor, and drank good Scotch even during the days of training; whereas other cadets could hardly afford rum or cheap liquor. His family's affluence made him more aggressive about the way he wanted to live. The Army never had any issue on how he wanted to live – but with what he wanted to say.

Nevertheless, Kohli was always an excellent performer at tests. That surprised everyone. Vikram was a contender to the top slot at the training, but Kohli turned out to be the dark horse. The instructors were also caught on the defensive and tried to dissuade the examiners, who had come from outside the academy. But they refused to oblige. The argument was that he had excelled in a fair and transparent manner in front of every one. And he had earned his honour on the strength of his competence. Vikram and Kohli were good friends. This, instead of creating jealousy or acrimony, rather cemented their friendship. Both had mutual respect for each other's talent and intellect.

They, however, differed in one key trait — the passion to serve in the army and its ethos. Kohli believed that life had to be freewheeling. He didn't want to follow the army's strict routines. He often said "in the army, even to shit, you have to take permission." His attitude earned him the moniker of 'Colonel'.

Kohli was called 'Colonel' by his batch-mates even during training. But after he left the services, Vikram called him

'Dummy Colonel'. He was full of life and energy. He loved solving puzzles and problems in life with equal ease. The best thing was that he was a dependable friend; the only one whom Vikram trusted with his secrets.

Kohli was also an excellent roast-master, witty and full of sarcasm. He woudn't leave an opportunity to poke fun at people. Rather, he would invent reasons to say things which made everyone laugh, without offending.

"Sir, you are still after my ass. By the way, I am proud of your bravery medal. I smile broadly when someone here identifies me as your friend."

"Oh, so at least you think I am better than you."

"Not at all, but I pity you. You are better in war, a great soldier indeed."

"My god, you leave me flabbergasted," Vikram replied in mock surprise.

"Come on, you chicken-hearted soul, how is life otherwise?"

"Not good, feeling lonely as usual but more so, these days." Vikram replied.

"Come for a break here, we will go for trekking and rafting in Rishikesh if you wish or something else. Or, do you want girls?"

"No, no dear, I am still a gentleman, unlike you," Vikram said with a laugh.

"Cool, I am more sinned against than sinning. But I am proud of this record, too."

"I know you, dear. You are the only one whom I can trust." Vikram was steering the conversation to a confession.

"Then tell me what is worrying you?"

"I am missing something …"

"And what could be that?"

"I think, I am alone."

"Yes, you are."

"Will I not get love in my life?" Vikram asked.

"Why don't you contact your Nisha, isn't she your first and last love?"

"Should I?" He wanted to be sure of what Kohli said before he made a move.

"Yes, you should. And immediately," Kohli affirmed.

***

Nisha and Vikram had always loved each other. They had even qualified for the MBBS entrance examination together. But in spite of her insistence, he didn't opt for medicine. It was Vikram initially, who was passionate about being a doctor. A passion that became Nisha's later. She wanted to contribute something meaningful to the well-being of the poor people. She thought it would be convenient if they were in the same profession. And if they wanted to work and live together. Different jobs could take them away from each other. She joined a medical college in Chennai, while he joined a college in Delhi. Once away, they both began to study seriously.

They were filled with the fervour of youth. They were busy pursuing their ambitions. Love was put on the margins – relegated to the back-burner. They were in cities far away and it was practically not possible to meet often. They spoke to each other on telephone, but mostly wrote letters. Both were fond of writing.

In her final year of college, she was under pressure from her family to marry her classmate. Deepak belonged to the same caste. Their parents were eager to fix the match. Nisha immediately wrote to Vikram about her parent's wish, and wanted him to take a call on marriage. But Vikram was in a dilemma. He wasn't sure about the career he wanted to pursue, and in the process, messed up the relationship. He went to

Puducherry on an assignment, but didn't stop for long at Chennai. He met Nisha for lunch. She was expecting that they would at least spend a night together. She was looking forward to the meeting. She almost turned her wardrobe upside down for a suitable dress, till she hit upon the right one after trying on at least a dozen outfits. She tried out several combinations of necklaces and earrings. Vikram was fond of trinkets. He had gifted her many over the years, and she was expecting a necklace and danglers from him this time, too. They were meeting after so long.

But the meeting turned out to be a damper. Vikram thought later. Not much came of it. Vikram did not sound excited enough. Even during lunch, he spoke about the work which he had set out to do and how important it was to him. She was a wee disappointed, but not hopeless. She tried to veer the conversation around to marriage a few times, but he dodged, saying it was too early to marry. He advised her to focus on her career first. He would settle down somewhere in a few years' time and then they should marry.

"Vikram, it is very difficult for me to resist my parents. I told them that I am in love with you."

"What was their reaction?"

"They were extremely worried."

"Why? Am I a bad sort?"

"No, not at all. But they think you have not settled down nor have any inclinations to do in the near future. What will you do?"

"So, you agree with them that life will be difficult with me on the move. After all, you will always earn well, isn't that enough for a family?"

"No, no, Vikram, I don't think that way. You know. For me these are not important. Only you matter in life. That's all."

"Then, wait. Let me tackle it my way."

"I am ready to wait. But the pressure is intense. You know my father has a heart condition."

Vikram interrupted her by asking if she wanted dessert. Nisha refused. He asked the waiter for the bill. As they left the restaurant, Nisha asked him to stay on for a day, at least.

"Let's check into a hotel and spend a day," Nisha insisted.

But he was adamant that he had to reach Puducherry by evening. Nisha kissed him passionately. It was not that they were kissing for the first time; the kiss was the staple of their intimacy. But they had never slept with each other. Was their physical attraction waning? Vikram was at a crossroad in his life. These thoughts forced her to wonder whether he was still the passionate boy she used to know; she dismissed his indifference as fatigue. His job as a roving writer was taking its toll – depleting his energy level.

He was researching for a newspaper article about destitute women on the streets – and their fates. And had been seeing only misery and deprivation around him. His indifference was unnerving. After all, they used to be so close, always.

"Do you love me, Vikram? Or you have started loving someone else?" Nisha wanted to know. Her voice wavered.

"Come on, Nisha, what are you trying to say? I love you. In fact, I can't love anyone else."

The next year, Vikram joined the Officers' Training Academy in Chennai to fulfill his childhood dream. One was to serve in the army. And secondly, to be near Nisha – the 'unforgettable forever'. He was done with wanderlust. But togetherness was elusive. The commitments at the Academy did not leave him time for Nisha.

On and off, she came under pressure to marry early.

8

27th March, 2020
3rd Day of Lockdown

Vikram pondered Kohli's advice. It sounded logical to him. Why he had not made any effort in this direction? She had divorced from Deepak a few years back, and was single. When her divorce came through, he was full of guilt. He blamed himself for not making it easy for Nisha with her husband. Their love was the stumbling block. The divorce had taken place seven years ago when Deepak left her to move to US. Strangely, he took the help of Nisha's brother to search for a job!

Vikram learnt about Nisha's divorce from a common friend. Still, he hadn't bothered to call her and find out about her well-being. He was ashamed that he had said 'no' to her proposal of marriage thirteen years ago. Furious and disappointed, Nisha told him in clear terms that for her happiness, he should not call her again. Vikram wondered why he had failed to understand the love and the hurt – lurking in her threats. Her violent reaction. Nor even, when he heard about her life after the divorce.

After Nisha's marriage, Vikram devoted his energy to climbing the army rank and file, but his personal life was chaotic. He did not heed any suggestions about it from anyone. He spurned advances of girls, who solicited his company. He neither flirted nor wanted any serious relationship. He was in no mood to risk being in love again.

When Nisha indicated that Vikram should not contact her henceforth, it was probably a cry for attention. Vikram didn't respond. He now cursed his poor understanding of the situation. Kohli suggested many times that he should have a formal relationship with her. He had always dismissed such suggestions as 'frivolous' or 'desperate', which irritated her rather than bring happiness. He always considered himself to be at fault for not responding to her call for marriage on time.

Nevertheless, now, he was sure that there was no other option.

His life was stale and he felt worn out. He did want to plunge into depression. Kohli called Vikram again to find out whether he could contact her. Vikram told him that he was mustering courage and waiting for the appropriate time to call her. He did not have her number, so he was unable to call.

Kohli retorted bluntly, "So, you need to be brave to call her, thank god, you didn't ask for armoury to do so." Kohli was after his hide to contact her because he knew it could change both their lives.

Vikram made many desperate calls to his schoolmates. The few that he could gather courage to ask about her didn't have her current number. He came to know from the school grapevine that she was still working at the Safdarjung Hospital. No one gave him her mobile number thinking that he had it. No one expected that the two, who were so close once, wouldn't remain in touch with each other, later. Probably, no one understood that it was too difficult to be simply in touch with a person, who was once like the breath that fanned your life.

You cannot have a formal relationship with a person whom you loved deeply once. It flares up emotions again. Love can't be calibrated. Love is absolute and its beauty defies cultures. Lovers behave the same way all over the world. Jealousy and possessiveness dominate love, too, sometimes to the level of insanity. But love is just that. And it is the way you feel it.

Office was hectic today. A slew of intelligence reports suggested that the Pakistani army was active on their side of the border. He had to revisit many strategies to enhance security.

However, Nisha's memories kept intruding. He kept recalling about her life as he knew it. She had a garden at her parents' university campus home. She was fond of flowers and tending to plants. She had wanted their life to be like the flowers in her garden. Nisha told him that she thought about him every day. He said that he looked at her photographs which she had sent him every night – and thought of her before falling asleep.

Their telephone conversations kept them occupied for hours, often at the cost of their studies. Vikram had to impose a talk time-limit of 22 minutes a day, but if she spoke to him for less than the time-cap, he was annoyed.

This was a different and difficult time. The Coronavirus was wreaking havoc the world over. Medical officers had never been through such dangerous times. There were already high casualties among doctors everywhere. In India, so far 50 had tested positive, mostly in Delhi. He was genuinely worried about her safety as she worked in a hospital, which was the first one to be declared 'specifically dedicated' to Covid-19 treatment. It was a Covid-care centre.

He searched the web page of her hospital for her personal contact number, but she was not listed. She was on the list of doctors dealing with Coronavirus cases. But there was no personal phone number listed against her name. It was possible that she might be genuinely busy. After all, tackling Covid-19 was taxing, time-consuming and unsafe. He re-read the hospital site to get some clues about the timings of the doctors and their roster of duties.

All the doctors were attending two hours' helpline calls in rotation. That was his only hope to connect to her.

Doctors were unwilling to share personal details. Vikram got into arguments with many doctors who refused to help him with her number. He toted his achievements and listed the honours he had brought to his country. He blasted one doctor saying that he had put his life in danger so many times for the country, and didn't his medals give him credibility enough to access the number of a doctor, who was on Corona-care duty.

He was on a merry-go-round chase.

Vikram was exhausted. He had been trying to get through to her since 11 am, every two hours, and it was now 11.30 pm in the night. But no one gave him her number. The 12-hour drill left him listless. Now, his only hope was Nisha herself. He was optimistic for some reason. It was 4 in the morning and if she was on duty, he could try his luck. He would steal a few moments to speak to her. The early morning was a lean period for the helpline. He had to take a random shot.

He couldn't miss the chance to connect to her.

9

28th March, 2020

4th Day of Lockdown

"Hello… is it…?" Vikram asked.

"Yes, this is the Corona Helpline." The voice responded.

He recognised Nisha's voice. He was nervous like a thief who had been caught stealing for the first time and was being asked to explain. His heart was hammering inside his chest.

"What to say? How to ask her for her mobile number? What to talk? How would she react? What she will do; humiliate him, snub and slam the phone down or she would be kind enough to speak?" She sounded so exhausted. Her voice was cracked, faint and mildly blurred. After all, it was 0400 hours in the morning. To make her connect faster, he thought it best to introduce himself.

"Ma'am, it's Colonel Vikram this side ..."

"Yes, Colonel, please let me know how can we help you?" She spoke in one breath, her voice drowsy.

"Not you all, only you can help me," Vikram said. Emotion made his voice quiver.

Nisha was suddenly awake. Had she heard, correctly? Was it Vikram? The same Vikram Rathore who didn't marry her. Was he suffering from Coronavirus? What happened to him that he was calling so late in the night? Was he safe? Her voice and thoughts became incoherent.

"Yesss," she somehow stammered.

"How are you, Nisha? I have been trying to get in touch with you for many days."

"I am fine."

"Umm," Vikram could not think of what to say next.

"How can I help you, sir." She asked after a long pause from Vikram's side. The prefix ,'sir', pinched Vikram.

"Nisha, I am Vikram, your Vikram," he replied.

"Yes, Vikram, but not my Vikram. Anyway, how can I help you?"

"I am worried about you, Nisha." He sounded genuine.

"Thanks, I am busy. Anything else?" She curtly replied. She thought his concern was fake. Otherwise too, it was useless asking and worrying about her after so many years.

"Please spare some time," Vikram pleaded.

"Yes, I could have probably, but not in these times. Bye." She was now angry.

"No, no, please wait …."

"Why? I have lots of work and my helpline time is almost over. The next doctor is waiting."

"Please give me your mobile number so that I can contact you."

"No use, I cannot take personal calls."

"At least, I can send messages on Whatsapp."

"Please don't insist."

Come on, for sake of our love," he pleaded with her.

She heard the next doctor asking her to move on. Nisha was confused. On the other side, Vikram continued to plead. She was a mess of emotions – a sense of betrayal, hurt and anger choked her voice. She could not forgive Vikram for abandoning her, not contacting her even after the divorce, which was the worst time of her life. She had so desperately waited for his call then. Why should she now share her number with him? What did it mean? Even if he came back to her, it would be of no use to her.

She was about to be 40 soon. And had learnt to live alone and was happily involved in social work. She was not in the frame of mind for emotional complications. Would it not make her emotionally unstable again? She had been through rejection, pain and humiliation in her relationship with Vikram. Why should she experience the same gamut of emotions again? After all, Vikram was so self-centered, he could not see anything beyond himself — his world was his own roll of honour.

However, she gave her number before she hung up.

Suspicious of himself, Vikram counted the numbers he scribbled on a chit of paper. Yes, there were ten digits. He had never felt so nervous jotting down a simple mobile number. It was more important than life itself. His hand shook badly as he took down the number. He struggled to write, wondering how all the organs of a body could work with such synchronised precision to jot down one telephone number. He could either listen or command his hand to write – but to do both at the same time? His thoughts were jumbled.

He recovered after a few minutes. He looked at the numbers, counted them again and felt a strange kind of satisfaction. He had not felt so content even when he was informed about the awards being conferred on him. After ages, it was something precious that he had achieved with great difficulty. As if, it was the numeric code from which he was reclaiming his life. He fell asleep with a smile. A weight eased of his head and shoulders.

When he woke up, he frantically searched for the paper on which he had jotted the number. He could not find it. He tried to remember where he might have kept it. He recalled that the piece of paper was on his bed under his mobile phone. He had slept off before he could save it on his phone. He searched for it everywhere — on the bed, the side table, under the bed and on the study table. He overturned the mattress and the pillows, pushed the heavy wooden bed to look for scrap of paper under it. He had almost given up hope, when his orderly came in to enquire what had happened.

"I have lost a paper, some numbers were written on it," he explained.

"Sir, do you have any idea where you saw it last?" His orderly asked meekly.

"On this bed, perhaps," distress was apparent in his voice.

"Right, Sir."

Now, the orderly started hunting for the paper like he was looking for a pin in the room. The way, he frisked the room disgusted the Colonel. But instead of sniping at the poor man, Vikram just walked out of the room. He didn't want to mock any effort by his orderly to find the piece of paper. He wanted the whole battalion to be tasked to find it. He wanted that number. He was confused about what he would do now. He didn't want to go through the torture of calling again after every two hours for two days, and wait for Nisha to come on line. Would she give the number to him again? Wouldn't she think that this was careless of him that he was not serious even now in reaching out to her. It was embarrassing. His thoughts were crashing into each other in his head. He was trying to think of his next move, when his orderly came out with a crumpled piece of paper.

"Is this the one, Sir?"

"Yes, it is," the Colonel exclaimed.

He felt like a man who had just been bailed out of a drowning ship. He saved the number in his phone immediately. He checked WhatsApp to confirm it was hers. He saw an image of flowers in the background of a nursery as the Dp, the 'Display picture', as her identity code. He was not sure if it was Nisha's. Suppose it was not hers. He had a sinking feeling.

He immediately wanted to send her messages, but restrained himself. He was apprehensive to break the ice.

On second thoughts, he realised that he could get hold of her only because of the pandemic.

Finally, he wrote, "Hi, this is Vikram here. Take care, see you soon." And sent the message. He changed his Dp, put one of his smarter photographs in uniform adorned with all the medals that he had been awarded. Reclining on his rocking chair, he thought how the circumstances had changed. He felt young. He had to wait for her to connect. And think before sending her more messages. Earlier, he would not even bother to correct the spellings in the messages he sent to her because she understood whatever he wanted to say. His boorishness and careless style of writing had always been his trademarks. Nisha used to like them.

He kept checking his phone for reply. Every now and then, he turned to look at the phone to see if there was any notification of a WhatsApp message. After few hours, he saw that she had read the message. She was still online. He kept his eye glued to the phone waiting for the status, *typing….* to appear just below her name . However, after twenty minutes or so, she went offline.

He was shocked. Wasn't he important enough for a Hi in those twenty minutes. What had life done to him? Once she used to respond at lightning speed. He thought it wise to wait for some time or she might be irritated. He thought of sending a good morning message, the next morning. A habit in people, he hated a lot. But re-connections were always unreasonable.

Maybe, it was the only way to remind her that he existed.

10

29th March, 2020
5th Day of lockdown

Vikram woke up late. He was not in a mood to go to work, but he couldn't afford to do so today because of the situation developing on the border. He called his adjutant to reschedule the operational meeting from 0930 to 1130 hrs.

He stepped out to his lawn, a patch of green with scattered beds of flowers. Few of them were in bloom. Floriculture was a difficult proposition in Drass because of the cold. Hooker's Irises were the only flowers that blossomed in early summer. These purplish-blue flowers bloomed amid long, narrow gray-green blades of foliage creating a striking backdrop. Traditionally, this place was known as 'Hem-babs' or 'snow land', *hem* meaning snow. Nothing grew here except goodwill. The Army protected this gateway to Leh and Kashmir from enemies and the local people often rescued travellers, trapped in the hail and sleet snow, on their way to Leh.

The lawn was barren and lifeless, reminiscent of the Colonel's life. Till a few weeks ago, in spite of the snow everywhere and the numbing weather, life was not that depressing. The Colonel had been in an introspective mood, albeit not very seriously. He was looking to find a purpose in life and this 'catastrophe' further pushed him into one. Often, he was nostalgic. He would keep thinking about what avoidable mistakes he had committed in his life and where his life took the wrong path. When you introspect, you find many loose ends and wrong priorities in your past. Not marrying Nisha when her parents wanted her to marry him because of his priorities at work was one of the wrong decisions, he thought. Perhaps, the worst among all.

He was still single. He decided not to marry after Nisha married. According to him, she had married too early. More than the family pressures, she was probably worried about Vikram's procrastinating approach.

When Vikram joined his training at the Chennai Officers' Training Academy, she had been optimistic. He had chosen the profession for a few reasons. It would give him the desired opportunity to serve the nation and the people. Secondly, he would be near Nisha during her last years in medical school and her internships. Her complaints about not meeting him and being serious about the relationship would also be taken care of. But the training schedules were too time-consuming and tiring. They were able to meet only when Nisha visited him at the Academy or somewhere nearby. Nisha was surprised why he had no sexual desire for her. They were already in their 20s but they had never spent a night together. She was yearning for the comfort of his embrace – and more.

After training was over, he was posted to forward locations in Arunachal Pradesh. Nisha's internship was over and she moved to Delhi to her parent's home. She took up a job on a contractual basis at the Safdarjung Hospital. She earned well. But it was difficult to hold out against her parent's pressure to marry. She told them that she would marry after completing her

MD; believing that she could crack any entrance examination if luck was on her side. But the mental preoccupation with uncertainties about her marriage cost her the opportunity.

Vikram, now completely focused on his profession, was almost unreachable. After his training was over, he was posted in Kupwara in Kashmir. Infiltrations by terrorists in this sector were at its peak. His unit was assigned the job to stop these terrorists from entering the Indian side. The job was risky. He had survived the bullet twice, narrowly.

Nisha called him the day he escaped a bullet. It was in February 2007, and what used to be sweet chit-chat once upon a time, soon became a bitter exchange.

He was aghast. She asked, "Vikram, you have to make a final decision. I cannot resist their pressure, any longer. My dad says if Vikram is serious about marriage, then he will marry me off to you, or I will have to settle for Deepak."

"Nisha, seems I have chosen too risky a job to keep you in peace ever."

"What do you mean too risky? You knew about it. Everybody knows about it."

"Yes, but it is about the time, dear. At present, I am a captain and will become a major in a few years. And the trends of cross border terrorism are such that we are going to face the heat of it."

"Vikram, don't speak like this. Nothing will happen to you."

"I know nothing will happen to me. But if something happens, you will be in a tight spot. You are such a vibrant girl You have so many dreams in life."

"All my dreams are with you. We have to see the world together."

"But my slot in this world will always be a narrow margin between life and death. This is the second time I survived being hit in the head."

"I have not imagined a world without you ever, Vikram. How can I live without you?"

"I agree with you, Nisha. Haven't I kept expressing my love to you in poems and paintings when I was not able to be with you?"

"I know, Vikram. It's easier to live in poetry and painting, but in real life there are many challenges. Don't shy away from them."

"Nisha, there is no life with me for the time being. I am not going to settle for any less challenging job till I breathe my last." Vikram was a man of strong personality, enough to change the course of history, he always felt in his heart. Yet, he was unable to understand the heart of a girl.

"Yes, I know of your dedication to the cause you are striving for and I am so proud of you," Nisha said. She took pride in the fact that she was in love with a person who was so dedicated. But she also knew that as a general rule any love should culminate in marriage. Sooner, the better.

"Nisha, I have opted for the para-commando resolute team. This elite team consists of tough commandos, who are assigned the most dangerous of operations."

"But your life includes mine, too. Did you consider that while opting for it? A normal course of duty is okay, but why do you always have to be in the danger zone? There are other people, too, and everyone should have their turn." Nisha was in no mood to stop. What about her passion? She has always known that chivalrous men desired pretty women. Was she not pretty enough to attract him? Self-doubts haunted Nisha.

"Why Vikram, why did you love me when you did not have the time to think of me? What about your compassion for a girl, whom you loved for ten years? Have not you deceived me? And now if you survive, you will be a decorated officer. Then, you will marry a general's daughter or a minister's daughter or into some erstwhile royal family of great lineage, who scout for army men like you with decorations and honours, for their girls." Her tirade hit him like hundred bullets. He toyed with the events of their past – over and over again – in rewind, introspecting, disseminating and analysing.

"Nisha, you are angry at me, you don't understand. I don't want to see you suffer alone, if I am maimed in battle, or I die."

"You are a damned idiot or a fool, who stretches his imagination to think of all the frightening things for yourself, just to avoid marrying me."

"Why don't you come here once and see for yourself?"

"What should I see? I have seen your name in the newspapers; recommended for presidential honour for your gallantry. You did not think that I was worthy enough to share in your glory."

"I thought I will share it once I got it. Recommendations are not final after all. It is preliminary – the road to bigger challenges."

"But gallant actions are worth sharing, isn't it?"

"I am going to dedicate this medal to you."

"I don't need your medal, I need you," Nisha was suddenly ardent.

"I too, need you, I love you."

"But I hate you."

"I love your hating me, too."

"No Vikram, this is not a normal fight where I say I hate you and you cajole me into saying that it is love. Now, I am really thinking that it was foolish of me to fall in love with you."

"No, you cannot hate me. We cannot hate each other ever."

"Listen, if you are not saying 'yes' to marrying me in a few hours, then you should forget me forever," she disconnected the phone.

Vikram was cold; he was not in a dilemma at all. When he opted for the para-commando resolute team, he was in a way sure that he would not trouble Nisha with his dangerous lifestyle. She was a weak-hearted girl and would not be able to find peace, given his kind of work. But Vikram loved the thrill of living on the edge; it made him feel worthwhile.

When Major General Alok Awasthy asked him to join the para-commando team because he could sense the potential in him, it was enough to inspire Vikram to opt for it. Not an exaggeration, as his career dossier showed that he fought like a daredevil. It's not everyday that you get such praise and motivation from a senior officer like Awasthy. Vikram's boss, Colonel Vinay, had soon made him the commander of a resolute team. He was highly tactical in planning operations, but the risk levels involved in his plans were always high. Somehow, Vikram managed to pull them off.

He soon became the blue-eyed boy of the corps commander and was decorated with the chief's commendation thrice. It was not that he had forgotten Nisha. But the success of the operations he planned went to his head. His swift actions foiled hundreds of infiltration bids, and killed many terrorists.

Nisha, by that time, was strong enough not to succumb to parental pressure, but she was not sure of Vikram. She was not sure whether the uniform had supplanted her as his first love. She had to take a call, she thought late into the nights when sleep played truant.

One day, she said 'yes' to marriage. She told her parents she could marry anyone; it was not important whom she married. She thought that it would be easier to forget Vikram and start a new life. Her parents had Deepak firmly in their mind. Nisha made one last attempt to contact Vikram before the wedding, but it was of no use.

***

Vikram's orderly entered his bedroom, carrying the cordless phone. It had rung thrice and he didn't pick up, so the control room alerted his orderly to pass the phone to the Colonel. He dialled his Lt. Colonel and discussed an intelligence report about the build-up of enemy troops across the border. The face-off was escalating into serious skirmishes, or it was probably a hoax.

Anyway, Vikram was restless. Unmindful. He thought about Nisha. He was eager to know how she was. How had she been coping with life? She was the only person he had ever loved. Besides his parents, she was the only one he wanted to take care of. He wondered how she was tackling the virus pandemic. Was she taking enough precautions? He knew that her husband had divorced her a few years ago and they didn't have any kids. Someone told him they had a troubled marriage. She could not adjust well; those snatches of news about Nisha played on his mind, almost 24X7.

Deepak had turned out to be a mercenary – and later, an alcoholic. He joined a private hospital, which was involved in unscrupulous medical practices. Nisha did not like it. She told him that she would not like to have children till Deepak mended his ways. Since then, she had lived alone. Vikram came to know from her friends that she had not been keeping well for a long time, after her showdown with Deepak. Vikram was at the forward posts. Mobile communication was also an issue and, whenever he tried to call her after mustering courage, she was not available on telephone.

From the bits and pieces about her life that he had collected from various sources, it was obvious to Vikram that she had been suffering all the while he was scaling new heights.

Vikram had received gallantry medals a number of times for his bravery on important national days. She must have seen him on TV or read about him in the newspapers. He wanted her to call him and congratulate him. Then, he would have dedicated his awards to her − and expressed his love. But the phone calls did not come. Vikram was hurt − or may be, it was his pride. The army website listed the details of the bravery award winners, she could have found him if she wanted to. The honours eventually began to mean nothing because Nisha did not respond. It was a paradox. Ambition burned like a fire in him − but the laurels felt meaningless without Nisha's warm gush of joy at his achievements.

In a few weeks, he even forgot that he was a decorated officer. What was the meaning of such decorations if he could not share or celebrate them with a person close to his heart.

He knew that she was moody and short-tempered. Maybe, she was waiting to be coaxed. Her hyper-enthusiasm, earlier, was an issue. She was very loving but it was also difficult to be her friend. She was prone to tantrums. Vikram could not understand whether it was her childishness or 'love-hate' for him, which stopped her from congratulating him or to contact him. At least, after her divorce or during the troubled times, she should have banked upon him.

Vikram was annoyed the last time when he attempted to call her. He sent her a text message, too. But she didn't respond. What did she think of him? Had she taken him for granted, then?

He had never married. Was it not enough punishment for a young man for not making the correct decision at the correct time? He was serving his nation at the time. He preferred to guard the nation rather than settle down to matrimony. Even if he had to die, he was ready to choose death. The cause had always been important to him. She knew him from childhood. Had she never understood him? Maybe, she did not ever want to understand. She was blind in her love and aspirations to a comfortable and cushioned life.

If it was so, then who would work for the nation. After all, isn't patriotism everyone's duty. Love for one's land was fundamental – after all, the ties were umbilical.

Late at night, he checked for messages once again, but there was no reply from her. He began to suspect that the number belonged to someone else. Or, was she deliberately ignoring him? Was she in love with someone else and wanted to stay away from him?

The questions were like a fusillade of battle fire.

11

30th March, 2020
6th Day of Lockdown

The news of migrant workers desperate to go back to their home states from Delhi and other cities was on every news channel on the television. They had assembled at Anand Vihar and Kaushambi bus stops in Delhi's National Capital Region and in neighbouring Uttar Pradesh in the last few days. In Delhi, there were widespread rumours – allegedly spread by the local ruling party that transportation was being arranged by the government to take them home. This was a serious a lapse to pardon. It was not only a violation of government advisory and 'lockdown' norms, but misinformation. Such mass movements could have serious repercussions, if the virus were to spread because of it.

Crowds of 300,000-400,000 had gathered for last two-three days, waiting for buses to ferry them home. Even if a few of these returnees were infected, they would pass the infection to thousands of others, who in turn could infect another thousand during their journey back, and in their villages – spreading the Corona like a chain. The media was highlighting their plight.

Many had no money, no shelter or food – and were without work. They could not manage to survive in cities. They were desperate to go back home. Many of their landlords had kicked them out for not being able to pay rent. Many homeowners just wanted to avoid crowding their houses and localities, and forced the tenants to leave.

When the government tried to force the migrants to stay back, they started walking to their home towns, which were often hundreds of kilometers away – sometimes in protest but mostly for fear of starvation and disease. Women holding infants and with kids, clutching at their hands, and men carrying their belongings on their heads were on their way home, in clusters.

Vikram checked out the situation in his region from the state control room. Drass, Kargil and Leh always drew migrant labourers from the plains to work on various construction projects. There were issues in that region, too, but not of a large scale. The home secretary of Ladakh had called a meeting of all the stakeholders to tackle the problem. Vikram attended it and offered to provide shelter and food in his camp to all such homeless people, mostly migrant labourers, till the 'lockdown' ended. It was the easiest way to ensure safety and comfort of this transient population with the medical staff monitoring their condition closely for 14 days of isolation, against the virus. Arrangements were made to send a few people back, if they were willing to go to Jammu. After that, such transits depended on the policy of other states.

It was a hectic day for Vikram. He had to set aside few tents and one barrack for the women. Food and facilities had to be earmarked. He read out the instructions and briefed his team.

But the most difficult part of the mission of was to make the workers follow the instructions. They were neither educated nor able to understand the damage, viral pandemics could cause. He entrusted one of his officers, Captain Abhishek to brief the labourers, who were sheltered in his camp, at frequent intervals to make them realise the gravity of the pandemic. He also constituted a team to keep a close watch on them and coordinate their stay in the camp. He asked the captain to screen movies on the projector to entertain them and to show them news broadcasts to educate them about the disease. News channels were relaying the Corona regulations round-the-clock and every journalist was striving to be a 'Corona warrior' with the latest update, countrywide.

Colonel Vikram, too, prepared a few pep talks which he planned to deliver to the migrant workers in the coming days to motivate them. This was the time, when leaders and people of exceptional enterprise, came to the forefront. Crisis brought hope and breakthroughs.

In the evening, the Superintendent of Police told him that the first positive case had been detected in Ladakh. So, precautions had to be taken. More precautionary orders were issued. The troops were lectured on vigorous enforcement measures, as more and more instructions from the headquarters and the government poured in.

Since morning, Vikram was on his toes but he was also in a contemplative mode, at the same time. He was cutting through the clutter in his head with a sharper focus. And it was Nisha. Her memory gripped him in the way the coronavirus had gripped the world.

Why was she not responding the way he wanted? Why was she not messaging or texting him? Was she so annoyed with him?

Earlier, when they had been together, she cheered him when he was angry or annoyed. She spoke to him for hours and mailed him her photographs. Vikram sometimes failed to understand her motives. Sometimes, her words made him feel that he was not her best choice. It used to worry him. That was why after completing college, he sought stability in the army. He had needed challenges in life to keep his confidence level buoyant, he did not want to lag in self-esteem.

Now, she was once again the sole passion of his life. There was hope and expectation in his heart today. Somehow, he felt that she would respond to him, but he would have to wait.

He took a break from his incessant flow of thoughts to spend time with his parents and have lunch with them. He had already instructed his staff not to disturb him on 'lockdown' days unless there was an emergency.

"The lockdown is like the black out which we had during the war," his father explained to him. "It is not difficult to follow. During the war blackouts, we were afraid of being bombarded by enemies, but in this one, we just have to stay at home."

Vikram was aware of the implications, but he listened attentively as his father pointed out the differences between the 'lockdowns' with great enthusiasm. His mother, too, joined the conversation. His father shared an experience that his grandfather had shared with him long ago. How Grandpa went underground during the Quit India Movement in 1942; it was another kind of 'lockdown'. Vikram was happy to spend time with them.

After a sumptuous lunch, they chatted a bit, and then napped. What pleased him more was that he was free of stress for several days, after meeting his parents . Once Nisha came back to his life, he would always be happy. It would be a complete family circle – Nisha, his parents, brother and his own self.

He checked the phone when he woke up at around 4 pm, there was no message from Nisha on his phone. He texted her a *Hi* and then asked his orderly for a cup of tea. He sat on the verandah, taking in the beauty of the mountains when he heard his phone ring. It was Nisha. He broke into a smile.

He was relieved that at least she had recognised him. She had written, *Busy, will connect soon.* Maybe, she was genuinely busy. It was a tough time for doctors. Lack of personal protection equipment and face masks were not the only challenges doctors were facing; hospitals were also short of beds and ventilators – and were crammed with unruly patients. The doctors bore the brunt of their anger and angst.

Vikram spoke to his parents for an hour over tea, the conversation calmed the chaos in him. Mental peace eluded him. He was letting Nisha's memories overcome him and was gradually becoming obsessed – frantically thinking of ways to make her return to his life. He wanted to sit with her, sip tea again, chat with her, go to bed with her and wake up with her.

He was meshed.

12

31st March, 2020
7th Day of Lockdown

Confusion had complicated the 'lockdown'. Domestic flights had been cancelled from 25th March, but evacuation from abroad had started. Air traffic controllers were needed to operate military operations but the staff was not able to reach the airports. Many of the forward posts in the Drass sector were air-maintained and coordination with other airports was necessary.

Most of the migrant labourers, homebound, were still stuck. The central government wanted them to stay where they were and asked the respective state governments to arrange for their food and shelter. Government offices were partially closed.

People were happy to be with their families but the fear of the pandemic clouded the reunions. In spite of the government's call not to indulge in panic-shopping, the queues outside the food ration outlets and grocery stores were very long. No one had any idea how the disease would spread. The states were active in their own ways, and so were resident welfare associations in the cities and villages. Schools and colleges were closed, so kids were celebrating their 'freedom' for the time being.

Television channels were broadcasting news related to the Covid-19 pandemic and how disastrous it could be. All other news were sidelights. Trivia. Inconsequential for the country's health meter. The worldwide figures were disturbing but in India, it was less so. Most of the people were cynical as to why the 'lockdown' had been imposed. The total infections of 606 on 25th March had increased to 1,397 on 31st March, a worrying spread.

The ringing telephone diverted Vikram's attention.

"*Jai Hind* , Sir. It's Captain Arvind here."

"Good morning, Andy. All well?"

"Yes sir, I have an idea about…," he was interrupted by the Colonel.

The captain said social distancing was an effective way to avoid infections in the battalion. The idea was quite innovative. Vikram told him to discuss with the adjutant and get it into force immediately. Encouraging him, he said, "*Beta* – son, God bless you. You deserve a dinner from me… just drop in any day when you don't feel like eating same shit in the mess."

"My pleasure, Sir, I cannot afford to miss the opportunity and I eat a lot. I am a foodie."

Vikram looked at his mobile phone for messages. Nisha had responded to his good morning message with a simple *Hi*. The good morning message was intended to please her. He was happy. He thought he could chat with her for a few minutes before she excused herself to prepare for her meetings.

Nisha had been to the hospital early because she had several meetings scheduled with the hospital authority and the ministry about the pandemic. He requested her to call between the meetings.

She didn't call.

13

1st April, 2020
8th day of Lockdown

The morning was not much better for the colonel either.

Late at night the day before, the father of one of the *subedars* – junior officer – had died and Vikram had to arrange for the *subedar* to go to his hometown. He got into action and spoke to various authorities.

No one was sure about the standard operating procedure to be followed in such a case. He issued a certificate in his official capacity and requested to 'whomsoever it may concern' to facilitate the junior officer's journey to his hometown. He was sent in a unit vehicle to Srinagar, from there he had to connect to a transit camp of the army and travel in another vehicle, arranged from there. It was impossible for the armyman to be present for the last rites, so he was advised to attend the rituals, following the cremation. The *subedar* was from Telangana, where the Coronavirus was spreading like wildfire, so he would have to tackle the curbs to enter his home-state, too.

Once the confusion over the 'lockdown' cleared, the logistical problems began to flood the public information domains. Hospitals all over India were facing a crunch of N95 masks and personal protective kits for doctors and nurses. Quarantine facilities needed to be augmented and upgraded. Monitoring was a huge task and an *app* had to be developed immediately to digitise advisories. Till then, Covid care would remain manual. Once a person tested positive on the basis of their travel history, all those passengers who travelled with the infected person were being warned about exposure to the virus – and advised home quarantine.

He discussed some new operational tactics with his officers to counter the increasing threat level. But for the first time in many years, he lacked coherence and there were critical gaps in the implementation plan of his strategies. He gave up. And told his officers to think of something better.

Trouble was simmering on the border, too. It was being widely rumoured on the Indian side that Pakistan was diverting the attention of its citizens from the rising Corona infections in the country by attacking the Indian posts. Such propaganda made the 'lockdown' enforcement more difficult for the army.

The 'Control' had informed him that a unit's forward post had been bombarded. There had been frequent violations of ceasefire in the recent past. Machine guns and tanks kept on firing through the night, almost everyday.

On hearing the news, Vikram moved his troops towards the posts and stationed himself with his soldiers. Once, he was near to the area, he could see the flashes of fire in the evening and hear the sounds of blasts at a closer range. The unit was used to such brawls; they had sighted their weapons, covers and *morchas* – positions – well, and generally, managed to repel enemy fire. The damages were superficial.

Once the firing stopped, they waited for some time. If the guns were silent for an hour or so, it was presumed that the skirmish was over. Vikram and his Major scanned the areas along the border to take stock of the damages later during reconnaissance patrols. He ordered a drone to assess the extent of the damage. One of his soldiers sustained a minor splinter injury.

After assessing the situation, Vikram returned to his camp late in the night.

Life was always running along the 'unexpected'.

14

2nd April, 2020
9th Day of lockdown

Once back at the unit camp, Vikram desperately hunted for a satellite-linked network to connect to. He first looked for a message from Nisha. She had written, *Gm…have a nice day*, in response to his six long emotional messages.

Nisha had called him while on her way to the ministry to attend a meeting. The Colonel was unavailable. He was with his officers, discussing inputs from an intelligence officer about the impact of the previous day's attack on the post. It was an important meeting and he thought for a minute about the next plan of action.

If he didn't pick his first call she made to him on his request, then she might not ever call him again. He looked at the wall clock. It was 1100 hrs. They were in a meeting for the last one hour. After the debriefing session, the strategy for next few days was being discussed. It could continue for one more hour. The attack had to be countered with a retaliatory strike and there should not be any loss of life on the Indian side. The report had to be ready by 1300 hrs and sent to HQ – the headquarters. The minister had to be briefed by the chief at 1400 hrs. Troops had to move at night and a preparatory command order had to be issued by 1500 hrs. He should not be wasting his time thinking about Nisha's call. The shrill ringing of his mobile jolted his thoughts. And he changed his mind. It was a split-second decision. He gestured everyone to leave the 'war-room'. It rarely happened that he had ever even picked up the telephone during such meetings. Discussions about security of border posts had wider ramifications on the security of the nation. He was re-shuffling the 'ramification' list.

Nisha spoke to him, as in earlier times. Perhaps, she wanted to bust the stress. The conversation was impersonal, mostly about things related to the pandemic.

She said, "You people will now understand that your cannons and tanks are of no use. We have more of that than the ventilators. Health care had always been a non-glamorous and neglected sector."

"I understand Nisha, wars are futile and don't serve any purpose. But we are only defending ourselves," he replied.

"Whatever it is, a big hospital like Safdarjung has a lesser budget than your unit. Imagine, you are in the business of killing people; whereas we are trying to save people."

Vikram did not want to confront her. He knew her perspective was not illogical. The world has been remorseless even after fighting so many wars. Waging war was a game of sorts and many loved it, except those who faced it.

Humanity hasn't faced anything worse than the calamities of war. Still, the reckless power-hungry leaders could never turn away from it. He wondered why compassion failed to influence people's reaction to violence, and their lust for bigger footprints. When Nisha's vehicle turned towards Nirman Bhawan, where the health ministry was located, she hung up, assuring him that she would call him on her way back.

Vikram was happy that she was making efforts to be in touch with him. It had the scent of a breakthrough.

She did call back, saying that the ministry had asked all the hospitals to prepare to tackle the Coronavirus. Hospitals needed to handle only serious cases so that other patients remained protected from unnecessary exposure and infection.

She sought solace in sharing information; she tried to keep the conversations as official as possible. Vikram wondered in whom did she confide in earlier. A person always needed someone to share one's thoughts with. In fact, sometimes you needed to speak out so that you felt lighter. That's why friendships were cherished. Nisha also described the impact of the virus in some European countries, which boasted the best of infrastructure. She was talkative today. But mostly about Corona. Vikram was not interested in news about the Coronavirus. It was all over the social media and on the news channels. Whatever secrets she thought she was sharing now would be released to the lay man in a few hours, the entire country would know of it. But he was happy that she had started sharing her thoughts. He just wanted her to talk and talk. Speak till there were no more words left.

He spoke to his parents before dinner. Back in his room, he went over their conversation, re-spooling it in his mind. It was such a wonderful feeling to associate with her again.

But his happiness was short-lived.

The phone rang and he picked it up, "Yes, doc, what's the matter?" The camp hospital was on the line.

"Sir, the man who was injured yesterday…"

"Yes, you mean Naik Mahendra…"

"Yes Sir, it seems he has some internal injuries and needs advance treatment. We have to send him to the base hospital in Srinagar immediately."

"Yes, but how? Our chopper pilots and crew members had been quarantined for the last 14 days. From where we will arrange transit?"

"I understand Sir, but it has to be done soon. We cannot risk sending him by road."

"Okay, let me think." Vikram was uneasy. The weather was inclement and choppers from other posts would take time to land and take off from Drass. It was not possible as night landing facility was not available at the airstrip. The choppers were positioned in such a way that only skilled pilots could take off in emergencies, but landing was difficult. The strip was hilly.

Though he informed his brigadier and the corps headquarters, chances of help were remote. He had to devise some other way. Calling a specialist from Srinagar or Leh was not possible as the roads were closed.

The doctor called him again and informed him that the patient was asking for water, which indicated internal bleeding that needed immediate attention.

Vikram went to the unit hospital and spoke to the patient, who was in high spirits, but sinking. Doctors ruled out evacuation. The roads were still full of snow and could not be cleared soon. A snow-clearing vehicle wouldn't be able to make way for an ambulance easily.

"Sir, I can manage this injury if guided by some senior doctor about it," the camp doctor said.

"Then do it with our doctors at the base hospital or R&R Hospital, Delhi."

"No Sir, it cannot be done with them because I am not authorised to treat splinter injuries as per Army's medical manual." The turf war between the various wings of the army was intense. These doctors at the headquarters would make everyone's life hellish, if the medical manual was compromised on.

"But, can you manage it?"

"Sir, I can probably handle it. Just have few queries."

The Colonel had to take the final call now. What was the risk? Was it worth taking? It was a big decision. On the ground, he had taken such decisions in a fraction of a second. Here it was difficult. But he had to take this decision on his 'appreciation of medical emergency', about which he knew nothing. He had to get his doctor in conference with a civilian doctor.

At that moment, he could not think of any other doctor except Nisha. But would she respond? Or, she may take it as unnecessary and unwarranted pestering by him. Whatever it was, he decided to call her.

He dialled her number. The ring went unanswered. He tried again. After calling her for the third time, he lost hope. Why she was behaving in such a way? He was not an idiot. He thought that she was a kind and helpful person.

Oh! let me keep my mind away from her and think of my man on the death-bed. Vikram started thinking of other doctors who could be of help. His phone rang. He didn't want to take any call at that moment. He didn't even see who was calling. The phone rang again and for the third time. Annoyed with the voice in the caller tune, he moved his hand to silence the phone when saw it was Nisha calling.

He was, as if, struck by lightning. Vikram paused for a moment, frozen. His hands trembled. He could not recall how to switch on to the call mode, momentarily.

"Hello Nisha. Thanks a lot for calling back. I need your help."

"Sorry, Vikram, I was busy with a patient. Yes, tell me."

"My doctor here needs some guidance for a patient. Why I cannot consult a senior army doctor is a long story which I will tell you later."

"It's fine, no need to tell the story. Connect me to your doctor."

"Yes, I am doing so. And talk to me sometime after this is over."

"Okay, I will try."

He went to the doctor's room and handed over his phone. After explaining the nature of the patient's injuries and the treatment so far, they put the phone on a video call. Nisha wanted to inspect the wound. Vikram saw her for the first time, in many years. She was looking tired and exhausted. She had pulled down her face mask to speak to the army doctor. She was clad in a protective body suit and glasses covered her eyes. Her face flashed in his mind, in all her moods as if in a frame. Her pictures in a doctor's apron from Chennai, which she had sent to him when she put it on for the first time. Then, she was an enthusiastic medical student – smiling and posing happily. Now, she looked like a grumpy old woman, tired and angry with the world.

Vikram's mind jolted back to the present when Nisha said, "Dr. Amit, arrange it fast and then call me. Hope you have understood my directions, well."

"Yes, I got it, ma'am."

"Okay, good. Then give the phone to Vikram, I mean Colonel *saab*."

With a smile of glee on his face, Vikram took the phone and nearly ran out of the room.

"Yes Nisha ..."

"Don't worry, Colonel *saab*, this kind of thing is my area of specialisation. You may not be aware but I have an MD and *thoda hum bhi pade likhe hai* (I am a little educated)." She uttered the last bit of the sentence in Hindi with a naughty smile. He did not know when she had completed her MD, but she must have done so recently as she had not qualified for it earlier. But why was he thinking about her degree, now?

"No, no, I know. I mean I know you are highly talented. Thanks for the timely help. Will remain grateful to you."

"Oho, will you be. Sustain this gratitude, Colonel."

She winked while saying so with a smile and ended the call.

Vikram was ecstatic. He had solved his problem so easily and so happily. She was called again for tele-guidance, when Dr. Amit was ready. She was methodical in guiding him. The surgery continued for almost 45 minutes. And the operation was successfully conducted under her supervision over the telephone. A life was saved because of Nisha.

It was also a big day for Vikram. He did not expect to connect to her in such a heartfelt way. She was still so amusing. The rigorous regimen had made her fair complexion pale, but she had managed to hold on to her health. In spite of being tired, she had pitched in with enthusiasm, like a true Samaritan. Her dedication to her profession was 'splendid'. He could not help but revere her for it.

He messaged her to find time to talk. She replied, *Not today, as got diverted in your work for an hour, so lots of pending work here.* The texts were like a life-saver for Vikram.

"Yes, I get it, still."

She replied, "No. Have mercy on me. it's 11.45 in the night and I have to eat my dinner and write reports about 10 Corona patients with complications."

"No issues. When you find time. Thanks a lot."

Vikram was satisfied with the chat. It was one of the happiest days in his life in recent times. He never felt so cheerful chatting with, or seeing a woman on the touchscreen of his cell phone, ever. It's not that beautiful women had not come to his life, especially after his string of successes in the force. Often in parties, he would be projected as the most eligible bachelor. His tales of bravery were narrated and he was glorified.

The Colonel was of average height – five feet and eight inches on bare feet, bright in complexion. Not conventionally handsome, but he was attractive because of his style, grace, sparkling brown eyes and achievements. He was articulate and witty. He dressed formally on official occasions but was otherwise extremely style-conscious. He had no one to spend his money on, so he had a lavish lifestyle. He indulged himself.

Nisha instilled a different kind of pleasure. She had always been a source of enormous joy to him. And, yet he could not feel this latent happiness till a few years ago. The demands of a soldier's commitments didn't allow him the space to explore the finer sensitivities of love – peel off human emotions, see through.

May be, love harmonises life better than war.

He could not sleep. Questions about Nisha bothered him. Why she didn't have children? How did she manage on her own? Where and how she was living? Who was paying for the household? Especially, these days!

He decided to text her at regular intervals. He wanted her back in his life.

A mission he decided to treat as 'Z+'.

15

3rd April, 2020

10th Day of Lockdown

"Colonel, called you to give some *gyan* – words of advice," Puneet Kohli's voice was as jovial as ever.

"Yes Sir, I am ready to receive it. It must be on how to earn from hoarding essential items and mint money." Vikram remarked with derision.

"Come on, you moron, I have enough money to feed your battalion and foot the bill to get your ass screwed."

"Oho, so it must be about war-craft then."

"No and yes, it is about war, but waging a war against Corona and not the useless Pakistani infiltrators, who will otherwise die of hunger, one day," Kohli replied.

He had a flair for research and analysis. And, whenever he learnt something new, he discussed it with Vikram. He knew Vikram loved to share knowledge. They spoke about the Coronavirus for half-an-hour. Kohli's knowledge turned out to be deeper than what all the news channels were speculating. About vaccines, prophylactic measures and the best ways to control the pandemic. He also asked Vikram about Nisha. Vikram told him that he was still confused as to what she had in mind, but yes, a connection had been established and he was holding on to it. Kohli cautioned him to be tender and caring and not bring forth 'his attitude' in this sort of fragile and loving relationship. The affair had its share of complexities.

Every morning, Vikram routinely sent messages to Nisha to call whenever she had time. Nisha called in the afternoon.

"Hi, Colonel, seems you are enjoying your life."

"Doesn't seems so, on what basis do you say so, dear."

"You came in my dreams yesterday." She told her teasingly.

"*Ahaa... achha to ab hum yaad aane lage hai* – so at last, I am back in your memory."

"What can I do, I have not allowed anyone to come into my dreams, ever."

Nisha got it off her chest. Maybe, she wanted him to know that he still ruled her heart.

She seemed to be happy today, Vikram thought. She said she had managed to eat well, sleep better and she had been able to buy fresh vegetables from the special food delivery vans marked to critical institutions.

"That's good, so credit goes to the grocery man, not this real man. Oho, my fate!" Vikram said in mock tears. They had cracked the icy shelf. They were on an informal wavelength.

Time was aplenty. Vikram had time to introspect and think about his relationship with Nisha. He used to think often in college that she was immature. Whenever Vikram would seek her attention or time, she would be busy in something else. But she bounced back to him, whenever she was lonely or was in any kind of trouble. Vikram could not help but notice the fact.

It was a twisted psychology. Whenever he was angry or annoyed with her, she would coax him out of it. She knew how to respond to his temper. Whenever he was angry, he needed attention and some sweet-talking. Vikram failed to understand her womanly wiles, sometimes.

Sometimes, he thought she was playing with his emotions. He was not up to the mark. He felt that he needed challenges to prove his worth if he was ever left alone. He would have married her a few years later, but he needed to 'go someplace' to stand firm on his turf. She was the only true love of his life.

The introspection tore at his carefully-constructed calm; fears from the past disturbed him. Vikram broke free of his thought chains by falling back on his parents. He set an early lunch appointment with them. He had already instructed his staff to not disturb him. The Prime Minister's appeal of 'social distancing' was a good excuse these days.

His father was waiting for him with his lores about the country's blackout years – from the days of emergency in 1975 to the other war blackout days, India had to face post-Independence. They chatted for nearly one-and-a-half hours before lunch; it strengthened the bonds.

"The 'lockdown' is like the 'black out' during the wars. And it is so easy to adhere to. Look at the advantages," his father laughed. His father had a habit of repeating himself. Vikram was ever attentive to his 'much-told' stock of stories. It was his way of reposing faith in his family, he wanted his father to talk. He loved the sound of his old and cracked voice. His mother, too, joined the conversation with a zealous zeal. She was more concerned about the depleted *bazaars* – the markets stripped of 'essentials'. He was happy to spend time with them. He had not felt so happy in the last two weeks as he did that day.

Anchors brought freedom in their trails.

16

4th April, 2020

11th day of Lockdown

Vikram kept sending messages to Nisha at regular intervals and she responded whenever she could. It was obvious that she was not ignoring his messages. She called him later, probably when she had woken up. She had returned to her own home after two days and was feeling relaxed.

She had started responding to him. Vikram wanted to talk about the past, their love and how he always missed her but could not dare to tell her so. She seemed to have become a Corona Warrior, fully dedicated to the cause. Vikram was happy with her dedication, but missed her as his beloved. She told him that her resting hours were highly unpredictable. Sometimes, she was free at 2 am and was too exhausted to even sleep.

"You can talk to me even at 2 am and I will see to it that you feel relaxed. I will take care of you," Vikram said.

"Yes Vikram, I need to be taken care of. I don't have anyone."

Her admission made Vikram cry that day. He thought he was responsible for the void in her life. Her husband had divorced her after six years of marriage and she had been alone for the last seven years. Vikram cursed himself about why he had not contacted her in the last seven years. What had he been doing all these years? Busy flirting with medals on the left chest of his uniform. Listening to people praising him and comparing him to the bravest warriors in history. He had won those medals and had been the hero of stories about bravery for last fifteen years, but nothing could ensure him the peace of mind. Nisha's desire to be taken care by someone sounded better to his ears than any citations.

It was a tough day for him. A brigadier was on a two-day inspection of the unit during the day and in the evening his boss wanted to see an exercise of war 'security scenario building' in case of an enemy attack. They had to move to the forward base. Vikram was worried as there was no phone connectivity at the base. Vikram tried to dissuade the brigadier to see TEWT – the Tactical Exercise Without Troops preparedness. But it was difficult to change the brigadier's mood. Vikram was at the receiving end of the brigadier's ire as he was getting more attention than the latter in the corps. A few of the brigadier's decisions had been overruled by the major general on Vikram's suggestions.

Success comes with many friends, fair-weather cronies and jealous fellow warriors across the ranks. Vikram knew the propensity of such people, so he wasn't surprised.

Vikram had to arrange not only the war-exercises but also ensure that they were flawless. He knew that the exercises would be viewed very critically. He had briefed all concerned. Being a professional, he would not compromise on them, but he was not fully focused either. While briefing, he kept on checking his phone. A behavioural trait that no one had seen in him earlier. He was a strict disciplinarian in uniform and did not compromise on the jobs assigned to him. Everyone noticed that his phone distracted him and he, too, felt that his fetish with the phone was becoming apparent. But he was confident by nature. His professional integrity was intact.

After a tough, hectic day in office, he came back home late. His parents had gone to sleep. He checked the phone for Nisha's messages. On seeing that there were few, he felt relaxed that she had not forgotten him. In an hour, he got a call.

"Hi, Vikram, I am so happy. I came back to sleep in my house."

"Why don't you come back to your home daily to sleep at least, Nisha." The warmth in his voice carried over on the phone, as well.

"It's very difficult. We have no time at all. We are all putting in extra hours as things are totally unmanageable now."

"But how will you treat others if you are tired?"

"Yes, but there is no remedy. We all have to work as there is panic among the people. They are restless even if they have fever and simple infections."

"Yes, the virus has created such fears."

"Agree, people don't care about exercises, eating properly, smoking and drinking, but they are really scared of the Coronavirus."

"Isn't it strange that in spite of a low mortality rate, it is proving so deadly."

"Yes, but once people test positive, they are unable to cope. They succumb to other diseases from which they are already suffering, like heart, kidney or liver ailments."

"Oh, I see."

"How are you managing your food?"

"Aha, so now you worry about me."

"Yes, why not, haven't I always bothered about you?"

"Yes, that's why you left me to pursue your own life of glory and glamour."

"Come on, that was the time I was confused and indecisive."

"About me? About our love?" She was genuinely inquisitive.

"Not at all, I was confused about myself. Never about you."

"And that's why you didn't marry me. For your confusion, you punished me."

"Nisha, I was on some dangerous assignments. There was low probability of survival. The casualty rate was higher there than the Covid."

"Yes, I know we doctors are petty creatures, can't understand it." She was sarcastic.

Doctors are not respected the way they deserve to be. It is fashionable to ignore doctor's advice, especially in countries like India, where self-medication is common. When a patient's condition becomes serious, they go to doctors to cure them within no time. They fight with doctors and blame them if a patient's condition worsens. Even bureaucrats treat them like their staff, Nisha's list of complaints was long.

"I get your point, Nisha. Doctors do great service to the nation but don't get the respect they deserve. But why blame me? I am in the same kind of service."

"Anyway, we are not going to crib any more. Enough. I am too tired and if you allow, I would like to sleep. Don't know when I will get a call from hospital."

Vikram was satisfied with the exchange, and felt they work the old vibes back between them. He extracted a promise that she would call him whenever she could. He kept his phone with him all the time. He increased the volume of the ringer tone and kept checking the handset from time-to-time so as not to miss any call.

17

5th April, 2020

12th day of Lockdown

Vikram returned in the afternoon from his field visits to the forward posts and company locations. Once back into the network zone, he checked his messages on WhatsApp. Nisha had written, "Called you, but could not connect. Tomorrow I'll be busy, let's see when I can call."

Oh, shit! Now she would be busy. The brigadier had spoiled two days. The roster of official commitments had been packed since the day he had tried to call her. Most were avoidable. Probably, he had not ever thought that way earlier. Work was his sole occupation.

He retired to his bedroom around 1700 hrs, tired and exhausted, but couldn't sleep. He kept thinking about Nisha. He didn't even get out of his uniform. He was disgruntled, thinking how the army regimen didn't allow anyone the opportunity to be oneself. If something had to be done, it had to be done now. Emotions, barring love for the country and the regiment, were discouraged in the army. With these thoughts, he drifted off to a fitful sleep. The strident and the insistent ring of the phone woke him up. It was Nisha calling.

"Vikram, I am not feeling well. The work pressure is very high. I am unable to cope. My whole body is aching. It's too much for me."

"Why don't you get some exercise from your physiotherapist to relax. That will at least give you temporary relief, won't it?" Vikram sounded detached.

"No, we can't seek help of any other person. In fact, all the doctors, nurses and the staff dealing with the Coronavirus patients are not supposed to go near any other person. Now, even our food is being catered separately. I am fed up with this nasty canteen food."

"God, why don't you go home to cook sometimes."

"I can't. I am left with no energy. And no maid can come."

"I can understand, Nisha but I don't know what to say."

"Yes, I know you cannot do anything. But my life is very difficult these days. You know I have always had a bad stomach. For the last few years, it has become even more difficult."

"I feel so helpless."

"Yes, for me you have always been helpless, there is nothing new in that." A sense of hurt and caution kept Vikram from opening up.

"Nisha, I could have come, but due to this Coronavirus, we are also on high alert. Our leaves have been cancelled. We are not supposed to go out unnecessarily to avoid being infected and harming the troops. They cannot afford to be exposed."

"I know, the army is your first wife, besides so many other hobbies, such as your girlfriends. Where in this melee of commitments, you will find time for old pals like me."

"No, it's not like that. I would really like to come and help you."

"It's okay, I was joking. What can you do? Nothing."

"But I can be near you."

"Do me a favour. Let me now to rest for a while."

Vikram was confused. Nisha's condition put him in a quandary. She needed someone to help her. Probably, Vikram could have been of some help. But the job was again making him choose one over the other. How could he defy orders in this critical time? He had already called his parents over to the camp. He didn't have any excuse to apply for leave.

So much was happening around the world. Every day, hundreds of people were dying and thousands were being infected. More than 37,000 people had died around the world, while around 480,000 were infected. In India, though only 83 deaths had been reported with 3,577 infections so far as the impact of infection had begun to show late, doctors were scared.

Nisha was not armoured against the virus.

18

6th April, 2020
13th day of Lockdown

People in the country were gradually assimilating 'social distancing', though many still defied the order. The restlessness had grown exponentially with the increasing number of deaths. The US president said that he would think it as good job done if the deaths were kept in the ceiling of 200,000 in his country. The US, it was said, had the best of medical facilities, yet it was suffering.

The checks were intimidating. Masking faces, no venturing close another person, frequent hand-washing with sanitisers – the triggers of this imposed cloister were like segregation. Apartheid. It minted good business. Unscrupulous traders hoarded stocks and sold them in the black market at exorbitant prices. The government even had to fix the price of sanitisers and the masks.

Hospitals were in short supply of protective gear. Many self-help groups came out to help. With better resources, private hospitals commanded more trust than the government hospitals.

But even with the limited facilities, the government hospitals were doing an amazing job. They did not refuse any patient.

Vikram became emotional thinking about the doctors and nurses at the government hospitals, and his respect for Nisha notched up. It was as if they were on the same side. She not only preferred to work for the poor, but had also spurned her ex-husband Deepak's suggestions to move to the US to earn big money. She was not money-oriented; most of the doctors working for the government were not. Money in healthcare was still a private prerogative.

"Vikram, most of the virus patients are rich. Since it has spread from China and then to Europe, the early patients were mostly foreign travellers," Nisha said.

"Why so, I think it is a pandemic?" Vikram queried.

"Yes, it is. But the origin is strange. Very soon, it will spread to the common people, when they come into contact with those infected; like their drivers, support staff and domestic helpers. But so far, the corona patients here in India are mostly elite."

"I see. You people are facing more tantrums."

"Not only tantrums, but they request to be sent home on a daily basis. They keep on insisting that they are fine and say they will fall ill because of the poor infrastructure and hygiene in government hospitals."

"Strangely, they are unable to see the good points. They only complain."

"Yes, human beings have this funny habit of complaining rather than expressing gratitude for the little comforts in life. They mostly complain about buildings and toilets."

"Agreed, when people use public facilities they leave them dirty and then complain.

After all, how many times can public utilities be cleaned. The S*afai karamchari* – cleaners – have their limitations, too. After all, they are also human beings."

"Well, how is Colonel *saab* so well aware about the plight of poor souls like us? We face it everyday. Doesn't the army ensure 'spick-and-span' washrooms and camps."

"Yes, we ensure it. But being a commanding officer, I know much the effort my clean-up crew puts in."

"You have seen how the 'Swachhata Mission' – the national cleanliness drive – was mocked by all when the government launched it. People thought it was government's duty to clean up the country rather than individual's responsibility."

"That's the tragedy of our country. Even good initiatives do not get implemented without political controversies."

It was 2245 hrs. Vikram and Nisha were on a video call. He saw a canteen staffer put a tiffin-box on Nisha's table. "My down time – dinner break," she said with a smile.

"So, you have not had dinner. Why so late?" He was louder than usual. The anger was creeping in; he was not happy that she was eating at irregular hours. It was taxing time and she needed to keep fit.

"Now, our hospital canteen is catering to all the patients and the staff. Patients are the first priority."

"Yes. I got it. But it's too late. I am worried about your health."

"Seriously! Are you? Then why didn't you marry me. You could have taken care of me in the best possible manner."

"I really wanted to do so."

"Which virus stopped you? She laughingly said. She opened her tiffin-box and began to eat, as she spoke to him. She liked being taken care of.

"*Chalo* – go, you have wasted a lot of my time. Now, let me do something else, too."

"Hey, come on. I wasted your time?" he said, pretending to be sad. "I thought, I freed you from stress and that, too, free of cost."

"Forget it. I will charge for listening to you."

"Okay then I give you this as fee." He sent her a flying kiss. She blushed.

"Seems that you are a habitual flirt. Don't you do anything else?" she asked. He could feel the love flowing even on the phone. She reciprocated with puckered lips, even as her eyes shone. The spark of love was rekindling in their hearts and it was precious for Vikram. He was desperately searching for the meaning of life – it could be love.

Vikram prayed for Nisha's well-being every day. Her hospital was a hotbed of Coronavirus. Three cleaning staff had tested positive, along with two doctors and one nurse just today. The pandemic had exposed the true nature of people. A few were grateful, but not all. Doctors and nurses were being forced out of their homes and apartments even in the middle of the night to tend to the infected. Respect for the country's medical corps had become requisition-based!

Medical bodies were advising health-workers "to treat themselves as if they were positive". Consequently, they were keeping away from their families, even their children. The higher work-load, coupled with the threat to their own life and isolation, was taking their toll. They were suffering from insomnia and depression. The level of stress was unmanageable. Doctors also had to deal with patients, who were scared and alone. No visitors were allowed to meet Corona-positive patients, who fluctuated between hope and despair, with health workers as their sole human contact.

The scarcity of appropriate resources, increasing numbers of positive cases and risk to their own life were not the issues that health-workers could shake off. They were probably the heroes for the scores of Corona-positive, putting up a brave front but inside, they were on the verge of physical and mental break-down. Two female doctors at the Safdarjung Hospital were assaulted. How shameful!

Thinking about their plight, Vikram kept fidgeting in bed. Sleep overcame him around midnight. He was still thanking the lucky stars that in India, the spread of virus was slow and would be over soon.

He was afraid that the virus could get to Nisha.

19

7th April, 2020

14th day of Lockdown

"Hi, Vikram, how are you?" Nisha's voice was hoarse.

"I am okay. And you?"

"I had less work today as the OPD was almost shut because of the 'lockdown' and the increasing cases of Corona infections. The overall scenario is alarming."

"Why, what is happening?"

"The disease is going to spread and many more will be infected very soon."

"Yes, but see since international flights have been stopped, we can expect some respite."

"Yes, we are doing much better than many other countries. But you know, people take pride in defying advisories. And that worsens situations such as these."

"I can understand your worries. It must be very taxing for you people."

"Taxing! We are sapped. Our human resources are depleting everyday as whoever is coming into contact with

Corona patients is being sent into quarantine. So, now all the unknown cases are being dealt with differently but at the same time, we are trying to ensure full care."

"I can see the time is going to be tough for you in the coming days. I am worried about how you will cope, personally."

"Even I don't know because our hospital has the maximum number of Corona patients. Once they come and are suspected to be positive, they are expected to be accommodated in the hospital. It scares me."

"Wish, I could be there with you during this crisis."

"No use, you will not be permitted to meet me or come near me. I am in a high-risk job."

"I will come voluntarily at my own risk, who will stop me?"

"I will stop you," she said firmly.

"Why should you stop me? I will come to help you."

"The way you stopped me once from marrying you because you were in, too, risky a job, similarly I will do the same to you, now."

"I know, Nisha, it feels bad."

"No, it doesn't feel bad. It feels horrible. And you must realise it." She disconnected in a huff. The memories of those days haunted her, when she felt left out of Vikram's glorious days in the armed forces. She could not share his place in the sun – her bit of limelight. Vikram pleaded that his job profile was risky. But he was not only alive; he was a decorated army officer, as well. Had she been his wife, she would have been sitting in the galleries shaking hands with heroes and VIPs in his medal investiture ceremonies. Vikram had deprived her of all those proud moments, saying she could become a widow any time. What a rascal!

Vikram knew that he had to take the share of the blame from her perspective. And, any justification of his past behaviour could only create more bitterness.

Vikram dialled back immediately. She didn't pick up. Her anguish was genuine, the hounding memories of the deprivation and rejection made her moods unstable. The pandemic was making people intolerant and angry. They were suffering from some sort of depression. Domestic violence had increased. Cruelty and brutality were so common, these days. He dialled again as he knew her temperament. She didn't pick up.

On the fourth attempt, she picked up the phone and shouted, "I don't want to speak to you."

"Yes, yes, I know. But just listen to me. Cool down."

"*Bolo* – say…," she said in a sulky voice.

"Listen, this is a tough time. Let's forget past and fight it out together."

"Yes, it's a tough time, but only for me. You are not facing tough times and hey, be happy. Corona will not reach Drass. You may even get a medal for protecting your troops from Corona." She didn't miss any opportunity to hit out at him. The suppressed anger of the years when he had not bothered to get in touch with her was simmering, coming to the surface…

"Yes, but your tough time is mine, too. It is our tough time. It is us, Nisha." Vikram tried to mollify her.

"Aha, 'us'? Since when? It's news for me. Wow! You cheater!"

"It has always been, dear."

"Oh, so love takes a break and then resumes. Does the army teach you such rubbish?"

"Nisha, please take care. Keep in touch with me."

Vikram could not sleep for long, he woke up in the middle of the night. He wanted to run to meet her, but the Coronavirus stood in the way.

20

8th April, 2020

15th day of Lockdown

It was a busy day for Nisha. The list of Corona-related activities was crammed. For every department, the virus was the priority. There was fear that many more restrictions would be imposed, like the possibility of further 'lockdowns' in the near future. Every government official had to prepare for the pandemic. The role of the army and the police was that of primary responders in such situations. Vikram, too, had received instructions from his headquarters to help the local government in dealing with lawlessness or in providing facilities and resources to the health department to ease pressure from the civilian departments.

Various protocols were drafted by a team of officers with limited knowledge, they had so far collected from the media and the Internet. Vikram had some idea about the virus because of his conversations with Nisha in the last few days. They had hardly chatted today.

Vikram called Nisha at lunch. She picked up the phone as she was about to enter her chamber. "There are now 150 positive cases in the ward and it is widely suspected that a few of us may be infected, too, because some of the patients had provided wrong information about their status," she said.

"But how can people be so careless about their own lives. They are more prone to succumb to the disease if they hide critical information."

"People behave in strange ways, isn't it? Some think they can't die and some think they are going to die immediately without any reason."

"Nisha, come on. Cut out throwing these barbs. Tell me whether you have eaten well today."

"Yes, I did. Now, let me prepare a case history of the patients before I go for a nap. Bye."

The Colonel was playing tennis with his officers, when his phone rang. It was Nisha calling him for the fifth time that day, though each time, just for a few seconds.

He waved to his officers indicating that he would not play further; and holding the phone to his ears, he walked back to his residence.

"Hi Nisha, sorry, could not take call immediately," he apologised.

"It's okay, Colonel. I am not going to leave you that easily. This time, you are in my grip."

"Aha, say in your arms – that is a stronger bond," Vikram said in a lighter vein.

"Colonel, you may be a gallant officer but you are shaky with me."

"I admit it, dear."

"What admit! You are not obliging me with this admission. In fact, for me, you are a deserter. You forget, you ran away from me instead of marrying me."

"Yes, I confess, I am your coward suitor."

"Come on, you are in a habit of praising yourself. Why don't you get it treated by some good doctor? It is curable," Nisha said with sarcasm – and also with love.

"Yeah, you are right. That's why I am chasing one of the best doctors, and a woman, so that I am more receptive to her advice and treatment."

"Hmm... Maybe, I am not the best doctor, but for you, I am the only doctor who can heal you. Who else will come even near to such an eccentric and grumpy Colonel? You are still unpredictable."

"This unpredictability is counted upon as good quality when you are facing enemies. Maybe, my professionalism overshadows my personal psyche."

"No, no! It has brought out the best in you. You have been your worst enemy, too." She paused and then added, "Does anyone leave behind such a beautiful girlfriend." By adding the second line, Nisha tried to mitigate the profound truth of the first one, lest he felt let-down. This crisis was not a good time to settle scores.

"Good, you are in a happy mood today. Keep attacking me if that makes you happy. But I agree, you are still very beautiful," Vikram replied.

"Really, am I? Even more than those with whom you flirted with after breaking up."

"I love you," he said emphatically, skirting any further talk about flirting. Nisha was behaving like a teenager. A young and suspicious lover. But did it mean that she had begun to love him again and felt jealous about other women, who tried to court him.

Vikram remembered when a girl had hugged him and wished him happy birthday in school, Nisha had been furious. He had pacified her and then hugged and kissed her. That mellowed her fury. The warmth and the taste of basic instincts had always been there like a latent chemistry between them. How he missed her proximity all the time. Had they been near to each other, he would have hugged her and let her head rest on his shoulder.

Even after all these years, he recalled how heady it was loving Nisha. She had a wonderful sense of humour and Vikram knew that he would be fine for rest of his life if she remained by his side, laughing and making him laugh. He drifted to sleep that night with those memories of Nisha.

21

9th April, 2020
16th day of Lockdown

In India, the number of infected persons had shot up to nearly 6,000, but the count was lower than some other less populous nations. However, in the US, the trends were catastrophic.

The first case in India and in the US was detected simultaneously on 31st January. When our country is compared to other developed countries, it comes off better; making the Army prouder. They boast about it happily. Everyone may not notice and comment on the comparative perks, but the man in uniform always expressed it. Vikram was happy.

And whenever he was happy, he wanted to connect to Nisha. It was the same during their days on the campus. They were eager to share their happiness and worries instantly, and if there was any delay, they became restless. When Vikram's first article was published in an international journal, he called Nisha to tell her about it, but she didn't pick up the phone. He kept messaging her, but she didn't reply. Finally, he wrote to her about his achievement, thinking she would be elated and would call back immediately to congratulate him.

But she was offhand with a casual, "Okay". That disappointed him. He waited for another hour, but when he did not receive any more calls from her, he accused her of jealousy. What irritated him more was that she saw the messages, but did not respond to them. Ultimately in despair, he went out for a walk – and smoked three cigarettes at a go.

He was about to light the fourth cigarette, when she called.

"Hi, Vikram. What all are you messaging me?" Her reaction was mixed; but she seemed more amused than angry.

"What all can I write. You are an MBBS student, while I am an arts graduate without talent and merit, not much to reckon with. No wonder, you have your intelligent friends."

"Oh, come on, what happened to you? I don't like any of my branded friends."

"Maybe, but you don't have time for me. And that's the end of our story and love."

"*Arrey* – hang on! And cool down. First, let me tell you how happy I am that you are an international writer, now. Let's celebrate first. Come and show me your face, touch it to the receiver and let me kiss you."

"No, now celebration time is over due to 'delayed response'."

"Come on, I was at the operation theatre with my senior doctor. Since it was my first exposure to raw human anatomy and blood, I was a wee nervous in there. The surgery took quite some time, and I have just come out . In fact, I am yet to enter my hostel room."

"But you didn't tell me anything about this long surgery class today morning, when we spoke."

"Because I was not aware of it. It was an impromptu decision by the head of the department."

"Okay, I take back my words. Have you seen my article? It will make you proud. Now, you can always take pride in the fact that you have not chosen the wrong man."

"I know I haven't chosen the wrong man. And I am always proud of you even if no articles are published or you don't do anything worthwhile. You are incomparable as a loving guy."

"Okay, thanks. I love you."

"But I hate you. How can you suspect me of liking anyone else? You have accused me of not sparing time?"

"It was said in anger. You know I didn't mean that," Vikram apologised.

"But I mean it now, and that is why I hate you." She disconnected the phone angrily.

Vikram kept ringing her, in sheer terror. On his fifth attempt, she answered the phone and cooled down after persistent coaxing. They couldn't remain apart for more than an hour. And, no prize for any guesses that most of the time Vikram had to cajole her – literally grovel at her feet.

She was still the same old Nisha. Proud and arrogant.

Today, she called back after three hours, around noon. Vikram had called her once he reached his office in the morning. She was tired and was sounding low. Vikram requested for a video call, which she accepted. He observed that she was back home, but the mask was still dangling around her neck with a stethoscope. And she was in her hospital apron. Her hair was in tangles and her eyes were swollen around the edges.

"Nisha, what happened to you? You don't look well."

"Yes, I am tired and bit feverish, too."

"Oh my god, is it the infection."

"No, I don't think so. My usual issues along with the body-ache," she said, coughing. Vikram had never been comfortable with her downplaying her own illness. Last week, too, she did so. He resented her self-medication even during their days in college. However, now she was an established doctor so he couldn't challenge her. He was concerned. He asked her to rest and call him when she woke up. He could trust her to treat others, but not herself.

She called late in the evening. He was worried about her through the day. Fever, cough and body-aches, including a headache – were they not all the symptoms of the Corona?

"How are you feeling now?"

"Not much better. I am asking for food to be delivered home and informing them that I will not be able to attend the night shift."

"Yes, good! You should relax. And just let the symptoms become visible, don't suppress them, so that you know what is the ailment?"

"Yes, I should better take care. You relax and focus on your work." She said 'bye' and disconnected the phone. An hour later, she messaged that she was going to sleep and would talk tomorrow.

It was a long night for Vikram. He didn't know how many times he checked the phone for messages or if she was online. Everything seemed to have been touched by the Corona.

The fear was pushing everyone up the wall. If you were out of breath, you thought you were Corona positive. If, due to change of weather, you caught a cold and coughed, you sank into depression and shrank into quarantine, wishing that the 14 days would end in a blink of an eye. And then you'd be relieved that it was not the Corona. The television channels were continuously broadcasting news about the virus. Even the movies, which were being telecast like the *Contagion* – based on the deadly spread of a SARS-like contagious virus, which became a pandemic. *Contagion* was made in 2011, followed by another movie, *2012*, which showed a demonic 'disaster' razing everything that came in its way.

Conspiracy theories were rife. Many in the army believed that it was a biological weapon unleashed by China. Some rogues in the 'Mandarin country' had leaked it – or it was leaked from a store by mistake. After all, China has always suppressed free flow of information because of state control. Such news otherwise would be damning for the country and China needed to block it at any cost. The doctor who had first raised the alarm was served police notice for spreading rumours and whipping up panic. Vikram was not immune to such conjectures.

22

10th April, 2020

17th day of Lockdown

Nisha messaged at 4 am, 'when you wake up, call me'. He saw the message around 0515 hrs. He called her immediately. She was still feverish, and was coughing even more.

"Isn't that a symptom of Coronavirus?" Vikram asked accusingly.

"Yes, it is. But I am not suffering." She responded confidently.

"Yes, I know you are not suffering. But why don't you get the symptoms tested. For my sake. I don't want to lose you."

"Okay, my chicken-hearted hero, I will get it investigated today." She said, assuring him.

Vikram relaxed a bit. The test would give her the time to rest till the reports came. Any Corona suspect was immediately withdrawn from work and quarantined, which was the standard protocol everywhere. The pandemic was so widespread that people lost their peace of mind with a simple cough. Reactions were almost obsessive.

China was at the global cross-hairs. Businesses were withdrawing from the country and there was a strong perception that it would never be 'the right time' to work in China for the virus could re-surface any time. The unpredictability of the virus was emerging in many new studies. It was asymptomatic. The test kits or even lab tests sometimes failed to show the infection. Even negative reports could not be trusted for long. The rapid testing kits which China had supplied to some countries were returned because of their failure to detect the virus. Both rumours and reports about the research about a Coronavirus vaccine were in circulation.

People with stronger immunity were less prone to the infection. But the young and healthy people were now being infected, the trends appeared to be changing. No one could put a reason to it. Even a few cases had been reported from the army and the para-military troopers, which was worrisome. The soldiers were mostly healthy.

Nisha informed him in the evening that her Covid-19 test was negative and she would have to report for the night shift. She was resting as her body still ached. Vikram was happy about the status of the report. He advised her to sleep well and, if her body did not rise to the occasion, to take the night off.

He picked up Gabriel Garcia Marquez's *One Hundred Years of Solitude* from the bookshelf that evening, to read. He didn't remember any of the story, he had probably read it long ago. He wanted to find out now how people behaved if left in solitude for a long time. What kind of behavioural quirks they showed and the tantrums they threw? What kind of tribulations did they go through? What dominated their behaviour?

Was it an indifference towards everything? Did the victims suffer from insomnia? Did they become insane? Changed?

He was not sure whether the book would have all his answers, but, nevertheless, the book was about love and passion, too. As the journey to Macondo had brought 'certainty' with its termination there; so, may be, his journey to Nisha's doorstep could end his solitude, his hunt.

He was not sure which was the right book to read. Should he read *Love in the Time of Cholera*, instead? Whatever! He had the entire collection lined on the shelf, almost new. He was not in the mood to read; rather he was looking for solace to justify the events taking place in his life, currently. He somehow wanted to re-assure himself that love could shine through such maladies – and win.

23

11th April, 2020
18th day of Lockdown

Each day brought more bleak news about the spread of the disease, in India – and abroad. What is known as community spread, India saw its mini prototype. In spite of the advisories, a large religious congregation of Tablighi Jamaat was held in the third and fourth week of March at the shrine of the Sufi saint, Nizamuddin, in Delhi. People from many countries converged upon the capital to pray. Even after the 'lockdown' was imposed, hundreds of *Jamatis* – pilgrims – stayed back there, including many foreigners.. And now, it was being said that almost 30 % of the new cases came from this single source.

Vikram was tense because the guard in Nisha's residential block – and many helpers at the hospital subscribed to the faith. Had they attended the gathering, too? If so, it was quite possible that they were potential carriers. But in the heart of Delhi, if such faith-based checks were carried out by the government, it would raise a hue and cry about communal bias. Nisha had been staying at the hospital's residential campus, which was next to the hospital premises. Also, she was hardly five kilometres away from the *Markaz* – the congregation – hotspots of Corona and near to many others. Thus, the people in the neighbourhood, besides the patients, were also in the highly-vulnerable category. And that tormented Vikram.

The restlessness, he was experiencing because of her health soon made him nervous because of the two pieces of information he received in the evening. First, despite the negative report, she was not recovering on the expected lines. Also, the Corona was not only often asymptomatic, but in 30 % of the cases the tests had shown 'negative', but the patient actually had the virus. A world which developed nuclear bombs and technology to neutralise missiles in the air was still clueless about the virus. Paradoxically, testing kits and medicines developed for Corona were not reliable.

Vikram knew that even if she did not have Corona, Nisha needed care. No one was there to look after her. Her parents had moved to Canada, six years ago to live with their younger daughter. Now, even if they had wished, because of the 'lockdown', they could not come.

This was the time when one realised that how much one's life depended on the other. Reports of suicide by those stricken by the virus were becoming more frequent.

Vikram could not apply for leave on any pretext except on extreme compassionate grounds. With the 'lockdown', the government had instructed the army and paramilitary services to not send anyone on leave. The unit had to be 'kept ready' to meet any exigency at a short notice. Vikram's unit was not only deployed at a forward post along the border, but was also expected to assist the local government as well. He was permitted to keep his parents at this non-family station on the condition that it fulfilled all his social obligations and that he would be fully devoted to work during this time of crisis.

24

12th April, 2020

19th day of Lockdown

Nisha felt worse. She was running a high fever accompanied by severe dry cough. She was resting at home after taking medicines for fever. Vikram connected to her on a video call and realised how ill she was. Nisha was lying on her bed in an untidy room. The bed sheet, too, seemed dirty and empty teacups lay in a careless heap on one side, piled one on top of the other. A basket of fruits stood on a nearby table. The table was littered with fruit peels. This, when Nisha was hygiene-conscious.

"What has happened? Are you extremely sick? How can you stay like this, in this mess?" Vikram was shocked to see the condition in which she was living.

"Yeah! A bit too tired to take care of all this, but will be well soon," she replied.

"No, you are very ill. Let me see if can I come to your rescue." He could feel her breathing becoming faster and shallower. Her face was stressed. He disconnected the phone and started thinking of how to be with her in Delhi. He could not bear to see her in such agony. Something died inside him seeing her in such a dishevelled state. He realized for the first time how much she meant to him.

He tried to persuade her to contact the hospital and run a Corona check again. She didn't agree. She said she had no energy to clean the home. Maids were not allowed in and, now the movements of the helpers from the hospital were restricted. He needed to go there now. She was gravely ill.

He mailed an application to his boss requesting a month's leave on compassionate grounds. He was restless after dinner, thinking how to pressurise his boss tomorrow to grant him leave. But, a sense of unease with the way events were shaping up –both in his life and in the forces -- lingered at the back of his head.

He woke up at midnight to the sounds of thunderous blasts. Not very far.

Oh! The bloody Pakistanis have done it again. The Colonel swore to himself.

His phone rang immediately to confirm his fears that OP-311 was under attack. It would be a hectic night. He connected to the various posts around to take a situation report. The posts were bombed frequently, but not with such intensity. There were reports of mobilisation across the border in the sector, possibly to pre-empt infiltration efforts.

This was deadlier than what the unit had anticipated. The attacks on the posts were apparently a covering fire to provide the terrorists, time and space, to infiltrate. The unit had lost one soldier in the bombings, early reports cited. But that was not the end of the story.

There was a *fidayeen* – terrorist – attack on the camp, as well.

25

13-14th April, 2020
20-21st day of Lockdown

Around 0500 hrs, firing started from the oil dump depot, barely 800 metres from the Colonel's office and his residential complex. The terrorists were hiding in the camp. The Colonel ordered tactical deployment of small teams to neutralise them. Three captains and a major led the teams. The young officers in the army were always full of enthusiasm. They didn't even need prompting to discharge their duties, a dedication which has kept the national integrity intact.

In the exchange of fire, there were injuries on both sides. A rough count indicated that five militants were holed up in the camp. Troops were firing with caution, taking care not to blast the oil depot as the flames could damage the nearby winter clothing store. But, the militants understood the benefit of the vantage and threw half-a-dozen grenades at the dump and in the ensuing screen of flames, entered the camp where a few auxiliary sub-unit stores were stationed. It was well-planned attack on the camp.

Colonel Vikram was monitoring the situation from the control room via CCTV. But the rapid exchange of fire forced him to change tactics. He went on the ground and kept moving to guide and direct his troops. The militants were heading towards the Quarter Guard. They had already damaged the stores extensively. Mostly, these *fidayeen* were on drugs. Their bravery was misplaced as they thought they could not be killed. But whenever they were caught, they begged for life miserably, like petty urchins. It was not the intoxication of ideology, but the 'high' brought on by the narcotics. Once the impact of the drugs lessened, they behaved like common criminals.

The operation to flush out the militants continued for eight hours. Tactically advancing troops killed the *fidayeen* – one by one. Two soldiers were martyred in the operation and seven others were injured. Among the injured was Lieutenant Colonel Amarjeet Gill, a veteran. It was a devastating moment for the unit. The unit had been doing so well on the border for the last two years. This route was not frequented by the militants and the Pakistan Army never openly assisted infiltration after the 2001 Kargil war in this area. It was a black day.

Many senior brigadiers and General Officer Commanding landed at the damaged post by the evening, to plan counter operations. Vikram could hardly manage time to speak to Nisha. She was not recovering. He told her about the leave he had applied for, and then, about the strike which made the prospect of his coming to her, so difficult at the moment.

After many strategic input analysis and terrain-mapping, a counter strategy was finally put in place. The ops was code-named "Op Coviding". It was Corona everywhere! The meaning of 'coviding' was explained to the unit. The attack had to be viral – like the Covid – to destroy the base and then the core of the enemies.

The colonel was entrusted to lead the operation. He was not supposed to move before 0200 hours on 14th April.

At 2300 hours, he returned home. He knew he would be disturbing her, but thought it prudent to call Nisha and inform her about the developments. She was at the hospital. She had been tested again and was probably positive, though it was not yet confirmed officially.

She had already been shifted to an isolation ward. Vikram felt as if a mountain had fallen upon his head. He collapsed on his bed in despair. This would be the second time in his life that his job would be prioritised over the love of his life. Last time, he had to forgo marrying her, but maybe, this time it would be too late. Who knows about the chances of survival of a Corona-infected caregiver? So far in Italy, more than 100 doctors have died treating patients.

Sleep eluded him. Even the armyman's natural instinct to rest ahead of an important mission, did not soothe him. He was awake, thinking of a way out to move from Drass to Delhi, which seemed a near impossibility.

His mind strayed and his thoughts returned to China. This was a new rogue country. Not new, it had been always so. China had attacked India without any provocation in 1962, when the Indians were celebrating the good vibes with the *Hindi-Chini bhai bhai* – brotherhood – slogan. That breach of trust should have vilified China, forever. But in 1955, it got veto power in the United Nations. This made it dictatorial in attitude. Chinese people had no freedom of expression and due to the country's large population, labour was cheap. By western standards, it was exploitation of human beings, but the world got cheap goods from the 'cheap labour' in China. Therefore, the word was 'mum'. Now, the world was almost under a 'lockdown' with more than half a million infected and over 50,000 dead of the virus, already. He realised that geopolitics was a mean game.

Chinese aggression or diplomatic offensive approaches with respect to Kashmir and Arunachal Pradesh had always been a pain for India. Probably, trade interests had not let India act tough. But, now the time had come. Vikram was angry with China. It had imprisoned him. The virus, from China, had now endangered the life of his beloved and had forced Pakistan to attack the Drass sector, for the first time, to divert the mind of its citizens, who were also suffering because of the Corona.

His thoughts began to overlap in incoherent circles. His mind kept spinning from China to Pakistan – and sometimes to the virus.

Had Vikram known ten years ago that humanity would have to face such a scenario, he would have left the army. He would have married and spent time with Nisha. Loving her, teasing her, helping her and, mostly being with her. He had missed the life of love, of being with someone whom you love. Going on holidays and spending time on the tempting sands of the beaches, in the lush green serene mountains and luxurious five-star hotels. He could afford everything, but destiny had charted a different course for him. How dry and lack-lustre, his life really was. He had no one to love or hold on to.

He set the alarm for 0130 hrs. But he was restless. At 0120 hrs, he switched it off and was ready in combat gear. He left for the 'war room', strapped his weapons, map, GPS, trackers etc, and headed to the briefing room. He was given a report about combat-ready troops by the adjutant and then he started briefing them about the mission. Briefings have a pattern. Most of the troops had already seen the area where they were planning to operate, so no one asked any questions, barring a few routine ones. The mission was launched as per plan and continued for 18 hours.

The task was critical and required all of Vikram's attention.

He called his Delta team commander Major Parminder. "Pammy, get over your fear and let's have some good results. We desperately need it. And make sure that your team delivers it."

He called another of the team commanders, Major Satendra Rathore, "Satty, by hook or crook, you will win the point beyond 311 Sector. You will have to push them back and chase them to their area."

The operational plan was drawn up meticulously. A fierce battle ensued. They attacked and pushed back the enemies with extensive loss on their side. Most of the Pakistani infiltrators, who survived the explosions and fire from the armoured piercing shelling, fled to their side of the border. Anything flying in the air scared them.

Fortunately, for the Colonel, none of his soldiers attained martyrdom, but several were injured. Even he sustained a minor splinter injury in his leg. He had positioned himself next to a half-broken wall when a splinter from a blast nearby, hit him.

The mission was a success. He called and patted Major Pammy and his team in front of everyone, "SHABASH – Bravo, you are a bloody winner, as always. The pride of the *Paltan* – troops. Keep it up!"

Back at the unit, Vikram filed the report. The injured were in the hospital under care of doctors and an officer of the rank of Major was attending to their needs. Vikram came back to the room after issuing necessary directions to all. He didn't mention anything about his own injury to the doctors as they were busy tackling serious wounds. He popped a painkiller, cleaned the mess on his leg with an antiseptic gel – and did, whatever he could, do to stop the spread of the infection.

Vikram decided during the operation that he would go to Nisha, even if he was denied leave.

Another 19-day of 'lockdown', the second one, till May 3 was announced that evening. He saw in on the television late at night.

26

15th April, 2020

Second Lockdown: Day one
22nd day of Lockdown

It was 2000 hours. Vikram was exhausted. His legs were trembling with fatigue and his head was reeling. But he needed to speak to Nisha. He called her to enquire about her health.

"Hi, Vikram, I was waiting for your call. How are you? All well?" She asked in one breath.

She was anxious after seeing the ceasefire violation reports on the news broadcast. She knew the area in which the violation had taken place. She knew that nothing would keep him from achieving his goal and if the situation demanded, he would save the lives of his troops, before his own. She didn't want to lose him, now.

"Yes, yes. I am fine, how are you and what about the report?"

"That sounds so good. Hope your mission was a success?" She avoided replying to his query.

"Come on, missions are always okay. Tell me about your health. Hope it's negative like before."

"Wow! You worry about me so much. Looks like you are in love with me. That's great. Say 'I love you' to me, only then."

"Hey, yes, I love you. Now tell me that the report is negative."

"The last report was wrong, it is positive. I am a celebrity now. *Dedicated doctor tests corona positive* ... haven't you seen the news channels flashing it?" She broke the news with laughter and, as gently as she could so that Vikram wouldn't be alarmed.

But Vikram was shell-shocked. He could not even utter words of consolation, or encourage her to face it bravely. He just held the phone, feeling dizzy. He was clueless about what he should do. He drafted a demi official letter to his General Officer Commanding (GOC), stating his urgent need to proceed to Delhi to take care of his 'beloved'. He cited his medals and decorations to prove that he was not shirking responsibility, even now. It was just a matter of chance that he has to prioritisze his personal need before the country's. He was clear about his priorities this time.

His GOC couldn't understand his emotional need, probably as the culture of services did not recognise any such 'relationship'. Those were the mores of history. Had it been the colonel's wife, the appreciation of the situation would have been different. When it came to helping its own officers and troops, the army could go to any extent to manipulate the rules. Obviously, an old courtship did not hold any water.

He rebuked Vikram on the telephone. "Hope, you are not a 'lover boy'. Love makes a man weak and worthless – like *Devdas* – the tragedy king." Instead, he advised Vikram to behave like a soldier and plan effective operations instead of wasting energy in writing missives and running away from the situation.

"Sir, I am not running away," Vikram tried to explain and protect himself, but he was cut short by the General.

"Yes, I know. You are a brave soldier but you cannot go and meet a corona-positive patient, at any cost. You cannot even go near her. And, if somehow you sneak in, then you would get the coronavirus, too. When you are not going to be of any help to her, then why are you jeopardising your life and a glorious service record?"

Vikram knew he could not convince his GOC. The General was from an older school of thought. Dedicated and disciplined. His had the army in his blood and was committed to his service to the country. He was kind and helpful to everyone. He would often motivate his troops, *"Battalion ki izaat ke liye jaan bhi chali jaaye to kam hai* — even if you have to die to honour the battalion is less."

Vikram waited nervously for a response from his bosses about his leave. Pacing in his bungalow, his gaze shifted from the mountains to his medals – and the trophies displayed in his living room. Honour requires many sacrifices. So many times, it had almost killed him. A thought flashed across his mind; when he could deal with so many combat scenarios, this was but an internal one, and would surely be easier to handle.

He received a brief reply to the request – "Leave denied to Colonel Vikram because of operational reasons."

27

16th April, 2020

23rd day of Lockdown

Success can make you arrogant. Even if you remain humble, the humility confuses you if you are unable to handle a tough situation. Vikram was traumatised. He felt like a condemned man whose appeals had gone unheard. He was hopeful about the General's benevolent approach, but his trust in the army brass had failed him this time. It was as if the work was more important than the man at it. He was not taken into consideration. Why had he served the army if he was merely a tool in the hand of a system to achieve some target. The thoughts hounded him.

All were aware that the Colonel was a great solider and at this point, his presence would be necessary for the battalion to control the situation on the border. People were expecting a victory, no further failures.

He spoke to Nisha. She was looking fragile. She had put on a hospital gown. The change from a doctor's apron to a patient's gown was agonising. Her face had no expression. She was on oxygen through a mask as she had been complaining of breathlessness for a while. Several life-support machines were strapped to her bed for the necessary treatment. Her speech was laboured and she was tired in a few minutes.

He was aghast. The stress showed on his face. He had googled to know the details about Safdarjung Hospital, the number of infected persons in Delhi, the recovery rate and every information related to the virus situation in Delhi. The mortality rate was generally 3-4% and even in the worst case, it did not exceed 5% in the initial stage in Wuhan.

He sought data which reflected higher survival rates. She was in age group of 35-40, which had the lowest rate of mortality. In the initial stages, it was tricky. Now, the doctors understood the virus better and so, the survival rate was higher. That was good news. More women survived the virus, another favourable point. Doctors survived more. Was it so?

Maybe, because they are exposed to different viruses in course of their work. They had natural immunity.

He prepared a detailed handing-over note of the battalion to the officer, who was the senior-most, next down the rung. He wrote different sets of messages and reports to his immediate boss, the Brigadier and to the one above him, GOC, the commander of the area.

He knew he would go down in the history of the Indian army as a 'disgraceful' Colonel. A soldier of his stature, a *Shaurya Chakra* winner – how on earth could a Colonel be so reckless. He was still in his uniform and cap. He glanced at the command baton and held it, probably for the last time. He saw himself in the mirror and saluted. His name was inscribed on the baton. He turned to see the roll of honour. His name was there. How proud he had felt when he had taken over as the commanding officer of the battalion – the most coveted post in the regiment. Every infantry officer dreamt of that 'honour'.

Looking out of the glass window, he wondered why people created their own prisons. The prison he had built for himself – success in war and failure in love. He was a human being and a soldier, a hardcore army officer; but somewhere, also a 'lover boy'. He penned an emotional letter about his convictions as an experienced Colonel. He remained in touch with his creative self in spite of his known felicity with the Kalashnikovs and cannons. He let them know that, "as a true soldier, he had learnt to be true to his salt and shed blood for the right cause. The ethical upbringing of the army exhorted him to listen to his head and then the heart. Death could not be a reason to run away from the person, who needed you. Nor, could any false sense of duty prevent him from leaving everything to be with that one person, who needed him the most."

He further added, "the regiment has many competent and brave officers, who can replace me as the commanding officer and some of them will do much better than what I can accomplish; but Nisha – though a doctor herself, can only be helped by me. Only my love and hope can cure her." He reiterated that "he considered it an act of bravery to be with her at this time."

In the last paragraph, he quoted from the Hindu scriptures, "the soul's voice is primary and it gets priority over all other calls of duty." He kept the letters and wireless messages on the table with instructions to pass it on at specific times. He told his control room that he had left certain instructions for the adjutant, and he should pick it up sharp at 1000 hrs tomorrow.

Well after sundown, he took out his motorbike, an old olive green Enfield bullet. He stuffed his credit cards, the meager cash that he had and a few belongings in his rainproof rucksack. Before moving out of the camp, he met his parents and told them that he had been given a secret intelligence-gathering assignment, and he was going to Jammu. He would return in about three weeks. He would meet them after the mission was over. His parents were not fully convinced, but they knew Vikram took on secret missions, off and on.

He saw the wrinkles on his father's face deepening further. His mother was nervous, though she didn't utter a word. They knew that it was impossible to advise him about anything, once he had decided upon it. They could see the rucksack on his back and he held the keys of his motorbike; thus informing them was just a courtesy − a mere formality.

They also knew that Vikram would not do anything drastic, or hurt anyone. Last week, they had seen how worried he was about Nisha.

Maybe, he was going to visit Nisha and was covering it up as an intelligence mission. It could also be a secret army sortie. They knew the code: *no questions asked*. Whatever it was, they wanted him to accomplish it. But they did not argue with Vikram any more, he wouldn't listen to them.

They had dinner together. Vikram ate like he had been hungry for days − and his mother helped him with several servings as if he was a child. He knew that food could be a luxury in the next few days. As well as the company of parents. He turned his mind to Nisha. It was painful to leave old parents alone, probably forever. He was not sure whether he would survive the pandemic, like any other person in the manic clutches of desperation − and codes of honour.

His worries were tearing him apart and he had a sudden idea, like a man being set off on a journey unknown. He hadn't thought about a 'will' or ever ensured regular financial back-up for his parents. He wandered around for some time, thinking what to do − should he write a 'will'. He went to his office again and passed online instructions to his bank to transfer money, wrote a 'will', and filled certain forms to transfer his salary.

Then, he revved up his bike and cruised out of the main gate of the unit; his actions were calculated, so as not to draw attention. A cold breeze was blowing outside. He felt free of the chains of the world he was inhabiting; looking to an unknown territory.

The sky was clear and the stars were twinkling to give some solace; some dreams and hopes. The sentry greeted him with a loud – *Jai Hind Shriman* – 'Hail India, Sir', which he proudly reciprocated. Maybe, it was the last time he would get such an honour and have the right to respond with a salute. He surveyed his surroundings once again. A black mass of cloud was hanging low on the dark horizon. He had this indefinable urge to return to the camp. From the chain-link fence, he could see his office, the lights coming from the tower *morchas* on the periphery of the camp. Then, with a shudder, he removed his gaze from the familiar contours of the camp, and rode on.

He drove cautiously on the Leh-Srinagar highway. Since it was night and a 'lockdown' was in place, he didn't encounter any vehicle from Drass in the outskirts of Srinagar. The road to Srinagar had opened only last week. Generally, due to heavy snowfall in winter, it took many weeks to clear the highway. But this year, luckily for him, the Border Road Organisation had cleared the snow from the highway in a record of 18 days. They had started early in February to clear the road from both sides. The biggest hurdle was usually at the Zojila Pass, which was cleared in mid-March. He took it to be a good omen.

This area was relatively peaceful – and thus had less military presence. It was a cold and airy night. He had put on his warmest army jacket, which was issued to the troops for extreme inclement weather conditions. It had a 'hoodie' with fur on the lining fabric. Besides that, he wore his thermal inners, woollen socks and leather gloves.

He wanted to cover as much distance possible before the sun rose. There were very few *nakas* – check points – either for security or 'lockdown' violation. Wherever, he was stopped for violating the 'lockdown', he flashed his Colonel's identity card and rode on citing 'urgent and secret mission.' Army officials on urgent duty come under the 'exempt category'.

However, his luck soon cheated him.

His bike skidded just before Sonamarg – and rammed into a snow-clad face of the mountain that was a natural shield on one side of the highway.

28

17th April, 2020

24th day of Lockdown

It was midnight, cold and dark. The road was covered with a thin layer of slippery snow. It was as if a fine layer of glass had wrapped the highway, making it even more dangerous. There was a steep slide – a sheer drop – to the left. To stop the bike from skidding to the gorge, he nailed it to his knee, made it pivot and swerve to the right side.

The slippery snow and the wheel that was stuck in the slush made it difficult to manoeuvre the bike. The bike skidded further and the handle almost touched the ground. The motion provided resistance and stopped it from slipping away. He breathed deeply, pulled up the bike, applying his full strength and then slowly turned it to the right on the power of the engine. He pressed the accelerator, and the bike revved up with a jerk, speeding for a moment and then collided against the snowy mountain side of the road with a thud – and stopped.

He fell down from the bike. It was dead dark. Away from habitation. And, no one was likely to pass by till the next morning.

Vikram got up, composed himself and then sat there for few minutes feeling lucky that he had survived. Then, he tried to pick up the bike. He couldn't. He looked for someone nearby, some house. There was no one. He was a few kilometers from the town, but didn't dare to seek help. Seeking help from the army or the police units could be risky as there was no reason for a Colonel to move like a fugitive on a motorbike at night. He should have been moving in a car or a jeep, well-protected by his armed body guards.

He had to rescue himself and move out as soon as possible. He kept trying to dig the bike out from the mound of snow it had sunk in. Half of the bike was inside the snow. An hour later, he managed to pull the bike out; thin films of sweat glistened on his brow despite the chill. He struggled with the engine for another hour. He was a novice in bike mechanics and repairs, but a few trial and errors worked like magic. The engine buzzed to life. He straddled it with a smug smile on his face – and drove on, satisfied. In the morning, he reached near Qazigund after negotiating Baltal, Sonamarg, Srinagar and Anantnag – covering nearly 250 kilometers in the tough hilly terrain. Vikram was driving to save his love.

He had been a casual biker when he had bought his motorbike as a captain in the army. But he had kept it with him all the time because it was the first vehicle he had bought with his own earnings. In Drass, sometimes, he would go for short rides. He was not a hardcore bike addict and did not know how to repair the minor snags. For him, biking was a act of liberation – a free run from his sins of the past. He thanked his stars that he crossed Kashmir valley without any major hurdles.

During the day, the police were more visible and he had to stop at several points to explain his journey. He has not eaten anything for nearly 12 hours; just stopped at a few odd highway kiosks to refill his water bottle and petrol in his bike. He wanted to cover as much distance he could to avoid the army checkpoints. He knew his adjutant would read the instructions at around 1000 hrs – and then inform all the formations in Kashmir that he had left the unit. The Army HQ could consider it desertion from the force, warranting disciplinary action and could even consider court martial. Immediate 'look-out' radio messages would be relayed to apprehend him.

It was 1200 hours. He thought it might be the time when everyone would have received the message. And especially, when it was known to the general that he could be heading towards Delhi, vigil would be tightened at Udhampur and Jammu. Not surprisingly, at the Udhampur Divisional Headquarters, many *nakas* had been placed. He was stopped by a captain, who was not convinced about his 'excuse'. The officer requested him to meet his boss, Lt. Colonel Bhardwaj. The Lt. Col. asked him politely about the purpose of his 'movement'. Colonel Vikram's reply was not 'tenable'. He tried to bluff but could not do so with a credible story. The message had already reached Lt. Col. Bhardwaj.

"Sir, tell me the truth. You are such a fine gentleman. Why are you doing this? I am sure it must be for some purpose," the officer appealed.

"Leave it. This journey is too personal and you may not understand it." Colonel Vikram said gently.

"Sir, but I do understand that I have to arrest you and I don't want to interrupt you." He was respectful.

Vikram briefly confided in him. Bhardwaj got up and saluted him. "Sir, for you, this is a noble cause. I think I can compromise on my duty. It is not anti-national and is causing no harm to anyone, except that you are jeopardising your career. Come and have lunch with me, freshen up, change your clothes and then move. All the army posts in the Northern Corps have been alerted that you have been kidnapped and need to be rescued. We all are on a mission mode to search, locate and intercept you. May be, because of your service records, you have not been disgraced so far. But you will have to tread cautiously from henceforth. You may be on your own." A slight change in mood brought a noticeable change in the tone of the officer's words.

Vikram agreed and thanked him profusely.

They ate together and then Vikram changed into informal clothes. Bhardwaj loaned him his jeans and shirt. An army officer's attire was not safe anymore. He also put on Mrs. Bhardwaj's white kitchen apron to look like a doctor and his daughter's toy stethoscope. He looked at himself in the mirror and thought that the change of clothes might allow him easy entry into the Safdarjung Hospital. He needed a new set of identity papers to travel through the 'lockdown'. He printed several fake identity cards on the lieutenant colonel's computer to drive through the 'lockdown'.

Bhardwaj selected one of the cards, went to his office and laminated it himself to maintain secrecy and handed it to Vikram. The officer then briefed him about all the look-out *nakas* placed on the roads up to the state border.

At 1700 hrs, he could move from Bhardwaj's post because that was the time when he could dodge some *nakas* during the change of guard. The troops on duty would be replaced. He could take advantage of the confusion. It reminded him of the movie, *Prison Break*, which he had seen last summer. It was thrilling and inspiring as he, too, was working on a mission. He didn't have any other mobile number, and so he preferred not to talk to Nisha since his location could be traced. He messaged her from Colonel Bhardwaj's phone. Assuring her, that he would be reaching soon and safely, and she should not worry. He crossed the Jammu border and entered Punjab at midnight.

One hurdle had been negotiated well.

29

18th April, 2020
25th day of Lockdown

In the morning, he reached Chandigarh, covering just short of 400 kilometres in thirteen hours. The roads were empty. Punjab was witnessing a spurt in Corona infections, so the vigil was stricter on movement. He was stopped. A doctor was given a 'lockdown pass' at the *nakas*. No one came too close to the doctor to verify his true identity. The guards were scared that the doctor might be infected.

His wanted to reach Delhi by late evening and at the hospital around midnight, when the guards would be dozing.

Vikram halted at his friend's house in Chandigarh. His friend Kaushal worked for the Defense Research Development Organisation. Kaushal, also unmarried, often came to his unit on official tours in connection with his research on defence products. He said, "I am a non-romantic creature and marriage will never suit me, so why torture a girl by making her my wife." His reply disappointed Vikram, who wanted to hear that not marrying was never a good decision.

In his early thirties, Kaushal's hobby was to sleep. Strange, people sought partners to sleep with, and he maintained 'social distancing' to sleep. Not bad in these times. Vikram divulged his reasons for escaping from the post. Kaushal immediately handed over him a PPE kit, sanitiser and masks that DRDO had developed. Fortunately, he kept a few at home for any emergency.

Vikram thanked him. After all, he needed the kit to make his way to the isolation ward of the hospital. He had thought of stealing a protection kit from a doctor at the Safdarjung Hospital, if he did not manage to grab one from somewhere.

"Vikram, it's good that you stopped here. I will help make your entry safe and hassle-free." As Kaushal was aware of the protocols, hospitals were following, he told Vikram about the precautions he should take while entering the hospital and going to the isolation ward.

Kaushal, a bike lover, also serviced the engine of his motorbike, when Vikram slept after lunch.

Vikram was ecstatic. His destination now seemed so near and possible. He had a sumptuous meal and slept for three hours before moving on to the last leg of his journey. No restaurant or even a *dabha* – street side food kiosk – was open anywhere for even a cup of tea. He drank water from the bottle and smoked occasionally during the journey. At every stop, he stretched his body to relax his weary muscles.

Vikram had spoken to Nisha for a few minutes yesterday. But today, he could not connect to her. On waking up, he tried again, and was able to connect to her. She was still pale and weak – and was unable to say anything. Her condition was deteriorating. She had to put in a lot of effort to open her eyes to look at him.

He closed his eyes, knelt and prayed to god. He reminded god how rarely he had sought anything from anyone, but this time he was begging. He was surprised that she had not informed

her parents or alerted any of her colleagues to keep ..
about her condition. After all, at this point in life, she ..
have confided in someone about her relationship with him.
was his fear of losing her that was dictating his thought process.
He blamed himself for contacting her, so late in life. And then
drifted off to a restless sleep.

He woke up sweating, fearful that some unknown calamity
had struck him — and the world. It was stuffy and hot. He drank
two glasses of water and sat up on the bed. Silent, perplexed,
he still sweated. On the side table, were a pile of reports and
statistical data about Covid-19. Kaushal was developing anti-
Covid products for health workers.

Kaushal came inside and asked if all was well with him. Vikram
nodded in the affirmative. Kaushal brewed jasmine flavoured tea
— a favourite of Vikram's — and served it with rusk, which too, the
Colonel liked. The biscuits were part of his childhood.

They discussed about the Coronavirus over tea. The whole
world was obsessed with the virus as if all other things had
ceased to exist. Seems, there was a pause button which god
had pressed, to confine everyone to their homes. There were
some good aspects too. Pollution had reduced. Nature was
regaining its charm. Street crimes had fallen.

He showered and dressed as quickly as possible. He
thanked Kaushal for his help. The help really mattered because
getting food outside home or even the camp for Vikram was a
privilege during the pandemic. He again thanked his stars. Good
friends and well-wishers were all around the world. At around
1700 hours, he set out on the last leg of his journey to Delhi.
Chandigarh to Delhi was 250 km by an expressway. With no
vehicles on the highway, it was tempting to drive fast. But Kaushal
had warned him to drive carefully as he had a lot of time at his
disposal. He could not enter the hospital before midnight. There
were stringent checks on the Delhi border. There was also a

look-out notice for the *Tablighi Jamaat* escapees. The number of positive cases had been increasing; and after the government was criticised about the exodus of migrant labourers, the state's borders had been sealed. However, after incidents of attacks on the doctors and the disrespect shown to them, the police were trying to ensure that they were treated well and allowed them safe passage. Vikram had to appear confident. This was the last hurdle in his journey. The Delhi Police was professional and could detect fake identities, easily.

He rode at a moderate speed. Thoughts of Nisha crowded his mind-space, her face haunted him. At the check posts, his responses were mechanical and thus, he was not detained.

"*Oye bhai, kidhar* – where to?" a burly police constable with a baton asked him authoritatively. It was the Delhi border.

"I am a doctor. On duty," Vikram responded.

"*Kon si duty* – what duty? Where did you go?"

"I went to meet another doctor in Sonepat." That's the only reply he could think of on the spur of the moment.

"Why did you go? It is not permitted. Hmm….and, now you are going back – entering in Delhi from another state. Breaking law for a second time. No doctor can do that. You seem to be too irresponsible *bhai* – brother." He hit his baton on the oil tank of the motorbike. Vikram could make out that the constable was suspicious about his identity – or reconfirming what he had said. His mind was ticking fast, thinking of a plausible answer.

Another officer approached them in protective gear. He could not even speed away. He adjusted his glasses and arranged his cropped hair, while wiping the sweat off his face with a handkerchief. Just to give an impression, that he was calm and was speaking the truth. He tried to use his confident body language to convey the message.

Vikram mustered courage. "I am a doctor at the Safdarjung Hospital and I had gone to meet Dr. Ashok Dagar to brief him and check on a Corona-positive patient, who was not responding well. I risked my life and you are treating me this way. Only three days back, two doctors from Safdarjung were assaulted. Where is this country is heading to? We sought protection from the Delhi Police, but since it was taking time, I had to go. See, my stethoscope and apron are still on me. I have neither eaten my lunch today nor slept yesterday night."

"*Arey bhai, bas kar, ab rulayega kya* – Stop, brother. Are you going to make us cry?"

The constable was taken in by Vikram's indignant outburst and expressed his gratitude. With folded hands, he said, "Salute to you. Please go, god bless you, Sir."

Vikram moved on, but the constable's parting grace made him emotional. He had lied to a man in uniform, it pained him inside.

He had become selfish in the last three days. He had broken several rules, lied at so many places and nearly deserted the army. The last week had transformed his life; of what he thought about life and the perceptions he had about the world. A law-abiding citizen and a decorated army officer had become a runaway, just to meet his 'beloved'. He reached the hospital at around 2345 hrs and sat outside on a bench in the hospital campus – to relax his aching muscles. He needed time to think and decide on the further course of action.

"Hello! Do not enter this building, the Corona ward is here." An approaching guard of the hospital shouted from a distance. Intrusions into hospitals campuses were rampant. Therefore, heavy security arrangements had been placed to stop the intruders. The guard asked him again to move out of the campus, immediately.

Vikram had no other option, but to comply.

30

Mid-night

18-19th April, 2020
25-26th day of Lockdown

Outside the hospital, on the Ring Road, it was difficult to hide without being noticed at this time of the night. It was a roundabout with arterial roads converging from all directions.

Even the pigeons across the road had stopped fluttering and cooing, probably because it was still dark or for fear of the pandemic. The silence spread around him like a blanket, complete and uneasy. There were no voices, no sounds of vehicles and a cloud appeared from nowhere, making the darkness even darker.

He tried to hide himself and his motorbike in the shadow of the trees, away from the street lights. Even in the heart of Delhi, one could find trees everywhere. This kindled a ray of hope. If trees could survive, then mankind could, too. After camouflaging himself and his bike, he wondered how to break through the security system of the hospital to enter the isolation ward. Security had to be breached flawlessly, he could not afford to be caught, now. The target was so near. He recalled seeing three guards at the main entrance of the hospital. He went to the back of the main administrative building of the hospital with his baggage and covered his face with a mask and a cap. He wore glasses with large frames to hide his face, camouflaged his casual civilian clothes in a white apron, carried the toy stethoscope and the ready-to-wear PPE kit, once he neared the isolation area.

He came to the gate and asked confidently, "Have you seen Dr. Agarwal going outside or towards the west corridor or has he gone to the Corona ward."

The guard did not know who Dr. Agarwal was. But they usually kowtowed to those who spoke with confidence, probably intimidated by their commanding ways. Guards had their own brand of psychology.

"No, Sir, I don't know, Dr. Agarwal."

"WHAT! You don't know him? Do you know anything here?" He stopped and pretended to be angry at him for his poor knowledge.

"Tell me, do you know where is the Corona ward or you don't even know that."

"Yes, Sir, I know it is that side," the guard pointed to a ward, and then added immediately, "We are not letting anyone go that side."

"Very good." Vikram said with appreciation, which brought a smile on the guard's face. A very old trick, but it still worked. Guards liked to be lauded for good work. He moved towards the ward next to the 'Corona Isolation Ward' and looked for a washroom. On finding one, he went and put on the PPE kit. Now, he was covered from head-to-toe. His fake identity card of a doctor at the hospital was not matching the real one, so he stuffed the card into the pocket of his shirt, but kept the ribbon to which the hook of the card was attached, dangling out.

After a while, he sneaked into the isolation ward.

There was no security guard in the ward. Due to the Corona infections, everything was safer nowadays, except for the virus. The only security issue was that these Corona-infected people should not run away and infect others.

The real problem was to locate Nisha among the patients. He had to avoid doctors or they could recognise him as an outsider. He walked cautiously, craning his neck and straining his eyes to see in the dark; to make out the faces. But the faces were a blur. The air was full of smells of medicines and germicides. He did not feel well – and coughed.

He soon realised that he had completed one round of the beds. But he could not find Nisha. So, he moved ahead into the connecting corridor and returned when the doctor and nurses on duty left the ward. However, he now had a fair idea about the way the ward was laid out and could guess where she might be. He peered at the beds which he had missed out previously, and looked at the treatment charts hanging next to the beds.

There was a feeling of emptiness, of neglect, as if this ward was lost and forgotten. A negative aura pervaded the space. Patients were coughing, and many were short of breath, gasping. But all were left to recuperate by themselves at night. Sounds of various life-saving machines choked him. He felt a lump in his throat. His legs were trembling. Had he been infected, too, and were the symptoms apparent, so soon? But he dismissed such thoughts and focused on his search for Nisha.

He found her name at last. He felt as if his breath had stopped. He felt the presence of someone, who was close to his heart. He slowly stepped forward to the bed. Once near the bed, he read the patient's name again in the chart. It was Dr. Nisha. She was using her maiden name. He was finally beside her – at her bedside. Pretty soon, they would see each other in the darkness. He gently pushed a thin white curtain aside to move inside and gazed at the head-end of the bed. He folded his hands in prayers. He had finally made it.

She was sleeping calmly, surrounded by an array of medical equipment and monitors. Like a golden bird in a cage. Most of her body was covered with a white sheet. Medical contraptions always made him curious. Her body seemed to be too fragile and weak. But, her face was tranquil. Her eyes were closed. The skin on her face was swollen, but her lips were wide as if ready to smile. He was seeing her after years. How many years! He could not recall immediately, but it must be at least after 12-13 years. There was pin-drop silence in the room. It smelt of disinfectants. All the wards were sanitised at regular intervals. He sat next to her and waited for her to wake up.

As if, a bell had rung inside her body. She opened her eyes as soon as he sat next to her. Staring at him, she whispered with a broad smile, her eyes wide open, 'Vikram…." She was shocked and surprised at the same time to see him at the hospital. She blinked twice, so that she could see him clearly and recognise him. The virus brought on hallucinations.

After making sure it was Vikram, she immediately understood the gravity of the situation, but didn't utter a word. She looked around to ensure that no one was present in the ward and then turned to look at him. Love flowed from her eyes. She slowly reached her hand out from inside of white sheet to touch him.

"Hey, how you could make it here?" she whispered.

"It's long story. How are you doing?" he asked impatiently.

"Don't know. Not much better. Three days ago, I relapsed badly but now I am feeling better."

"Don't worry, you will recover fast now."

"Oh! Yes. My lord, my love has reached and now god has ordained to make things better for me," she joked, feeling better in his presence.

"Yes, it will be better." He said with confidence. Now, he had to help her with love and care. He enquired about the routine of the hospital and the visits by the teams of doctors, the probable hiding places and the timings so that he could visit her, without being caught. He sat with her till five in the morning, reassuring her. Filling her on the gaps.

Nisha gave him the key to her house. He wanted to know from her whether he could sleep in her bedroom to get a feel of her. She nodded, but warned that her bedroom might be infected. Words sapped her, so she asked Vikram to steer the conversation. She would prefer to listen. When he touched her hand, she was overwhelmed. It was like the Midas touch. She forgot the rules. Vikram could also be infected by the virus. She was caught in the moment. And that moment had no future and no past!

31

19th April, 2020
26th day of Lockdown

Early in the morning, before the sun rose on the misty capital, he left the hospital for her home. He had to assure the security guard that he got the keys from her; and that he was a relative, and not a trespasser.

Once inside, he took a quick tour of the apartment. He was curious to know how she lived, what she ate, where she drank her morning tea.... He took in the colour of the walls, the decorations and her pictures. The sight of her bed stirred something deep in him.. He examined everything with curiosity, like a child on a familiarisation tour. She had a mini-library in her bedroom. Books were stacked in a glass *almirah* with wooden frames, and in front of it was a rocking chair with a footstool. The chair had an off-white upholstery with a small red cushion. Besides the chair was a side table. There was a charging point near the table. This arrangement was near the terrace. The curtains were red and white. The bed was king-size, and next to it was her wardrobe. He saw rows of fashionable designer clothes stacked on the hangers and piles of simpler ones. In another shelf, he noticed her aprons, gloves and the equipment, she needed as a doctor.

Her undergarments were stacked in the middle shelf of the wardrobe. He wanted to feel them, but thought it was not prudent to do so and hastily closed the door of the wardrobe. He felt Nisha's physical presence in the room.

Before he left the hospital, Nisha had said, "Go, see my house and how I lived my life all these years." Probably she wanted to add 'without you', but refrained from saying so. Maybe, she would say so when they had enough time to catch up, later.

Suddenly, he recalled her warning to sanitise the home properly. She had instructed him how to do it. The hospital had provided its crew a can of sodium hypo-chlorite solution which was to be mixed with water, diluted and sprayed. He looked for it in a bedroom which seemed to double as a store room, too. It was damp and stank of something fetid.

The house was untidy. He cleaned it. The task took him two hours. He re-arranged the furniture so that she could get a feel of his own brand of aesthetics, on her return. That was when he felt the sharp stabs of hunger – like fiery aches in the pit of his stomach. He realised that he had not eaten anything since morning. Exhaustion made him numb or perhaps – hyper-active. He switched on the television, scanning the channels. Then he had a bath, made tea which he drank with some rather stale bread, he found in the refrigerator.

Nisha told him to visit her at 2 pm as there were very few attendants and guards in the hospital then, and the Corona ward was almost empty. He entered the isolation ward more confidently, this time. He carried some snacks which she had requested. He could see her face more clearly, in the daylight. Her hair was untidy, but looked good when it fell on her broad forehead in unruly locks. Her sharp nose appeared to be tinged with pink. Maybe, because her cheeks were so pale. She wore small gold earrings and a necklace.

"You are looking young and more handsome, Vikram." She looked at him with maternal kindness.

She was fed up of being confined to the bed. Her vitals were normal at the moment. She had been to the Intensive Care Unit (ICU) twice, and once on the ventilator. She was recovering, but the condition of the Corona patients was always unpredictable, swelling and ebbing.

Nisha suddenly realised that Vikram would also be infected soon or may have been infected, already. He was still holding her hand in his and the feeling was so good that she didn't want to take it back. But a strange sadness dimmed the glow in her eyes.

"Vikram, I couldn't give you my love, but I must have easily transmitted my disease." Tears filled her eyes. How casual and selfish she had been yesterday. She was surprised how she could be like that. Had she lost her senses on seeing Vikram? Or it was some kind of metamorphosis? Corona had, it seems, decimated her sensibilities.

Nisha had been suggesting social distancing to everyone for the last few weeks, but when it came to the person she wanted to protect the most, she gave in to her human frailties. She felt dejected. Since her ailment began, she was often overcome with emotions, swinging between hope and despair. Vikram's arrival had made her happy but this *faux pas* could be dangerous. Vikram understood her dilemma.

Back in her home, Vikram went to her bedroom. He would go to the hospital around midnight for a few hours. He decided to sleep on her bed. The moment he lay down on the bed, he felt as if she was speaking to him. She must have been lonely, sleeping alone, without a companion. She must have cried here when her husband left her. She must have been here, sick and helpless. He saw a pillow. She possibly clutched at it during the lonely winter nights. He hugged it to his body. It was like loving her. The pillows in his bedroom didn't give him the same feelings – they felt like his duty roster.

He removed his glasses and put them on the side table. He saw some papers there and a gel-pen. The pen was still open. She was writing something. He picked up a sheet.

Nisha had wasted several sheets of paper trying to frame a letter, 'Dear Vikram ....' and one or two more lines, addressing him. She had attempted to write to him many times, but could not proceed beyond a line or two. Those few words reflected the anguish of her loneliness, especially without him. He was restless and got up from the bed. What books did she read? There were Murakami, Kafka, Camus, Gabriel Marquez etc... He stood still when saw Murakami's *Men without Women*. Probably, she was trying to understand a man's life, demystify it. And that may have been the reason why she could not ever write a letter to him. His analysis ran into strange inferences.

He stepped back and stared at everything as if he had entered his own room after years. Half the memories of his life were here. Memories of the days, he had missed. Like the book, wide open. Like a play, about to enact. The scenes had been written, but were waiting to unfold. The missed chapters of his life. Missed dialogues!. The more he walked around the home, the more he felt as if he was turning the pages of the book.

He opened the wardrobe. He looked again at her dresses and imagined that how she would have looked in them. He appreciated them but the thought would not be able to do justice without seeing her in them. There were dresses in red and pink, black and indigo. But most were in shades of white or cream. He opened the shelf, where her undergarments were stacked. He touched them with hesitation and then pulled all of them out. She owned several many fashionable and colourful lingerie but they did not look worn or used often. Oh! She has not been doing justice to her body. Why did she deprive herself of the beauty that she possessed.

That night, both were more composed. Nisha was wondering why Vikram came to her now when she was dying. A bit of company and 'I love you' would have been enough. Even the bodies of the Corona patients are not handed over to the relatives lest it spread from there. He told her that he had come to help her tide over her suffering – to heal her.

"I have not come to die here, Nisha. I have come here to live with you and be with you in afterlife, too."

"But Vikram, why should you die with me, I won't survive for years but for few days, only. You are healthy and can live for decades."

"I had already lived many years and now those few days will be the most precious in my life." Vikram was firm and passionate.

"So, you are in the *fidayeen* mode here?".

"Whatever".

"Then let me elope with you. Take me away from this seedy place." She was as emotional; and suddenly very reckless.

He was silent. He saw two nurses approaching them, and melted into the shadows.

32

20th April, 2020

27th day of Lockdown

Vikram returned to her flat. Nisha's words kept haunting him. It was already 0500 hours. He went to the balcony and sat there with a mug of green tea. Maybe, the rising sun would enlighten him. Would it be appropriate to take her out of critical care? Would she survive? Or, did she want to live the few hours left in her life on her own terms? What would be the best thing to do?

She had always been an enigma to him. She thought fast and wanted to accomplish her goals, faster. He wanted to fulfill her wish. He felt the sadness washing over him like waves. It could expedite her death.

Taking a logical decision about those you love is never easy. He sat there for two hours. The sun shone brightly. April in Delhi could get pretty warm. This was quite a contrast to the chilly Drass, where the sun took a long time to seep through the ice.

Vikram wanted to consult someone. He could not think of any other person except Kohli. He called him, but Kolhi didn't reply. After waiting for a while for Kohli to call back, he went to sleep.

Later, he woke up to a tiny, familiar ring. Puneet Kohli was calling.

"I trust nothing is wrong," Kohli asked.

"Not much so far, except that I ran away from the army and now Nisha wants to run away with me." He narrated the whole story in brief and sought Kohli's opinion.

"Wonderful! Finally, you have done it. I think she is seriously ill and may not survive. Give her a few days of love."

"Will it be ethical?"

"I assume."

"How helpless I will be if I get infected, too." Vikram was skeptical.

"Think of it this way, may be god has given you an opportunity for penance even if you suffer."

Kohli was happily-married to his childhood sweetheart Ridhima. They had been in love since the day they met in Class 8. One of the reasons why Kohli left his job in the army was that they could not live away from each other.

Kohli always thought Vikram's life was too inert and dispassionate.

Vikram went to meet Nisha in the afternoon. He tried to gauge her thoughts – and find out whether she really wanted to get out of the hospital. Was she really contemplating running away? He guessed that she was fed up with the isolation ward. She just wanted to be on her own in the last few days. She was sure she wouldn't survive and told him that nothing rejuvenated her except his touch. She whispered while holding his hand, "It feels good being with you. I am lucky to have you."

"It's 'we'. Why don't you learn the grammar of love!"

33

21st April, 2020

28th day of Lockdown

The hospital had several review meetings scheduled for the day, and very few doctors were present in the wards that morning. When the doctors were not around, the attendants and the paramedics idled away, and by noon the wards were almost deserted.

Nisha wondered why Vikram wasn't there. What could have happened to him? Was he down with the Corona, too? Had he been caught and handed over to the police or had he run away again, after weighing the cons and pros?

Her thoughts were not baseless. She feared the worst, but waited for his usual arrival time at noon. He didn't turn up. By 4 pm she was despondent; but still refused to give up hope even as her sanity played the traitor, filling her with insidious possibilities. Why did he have to come into her life like this and then disappear? Why did he try to kindle hope in a dying soul? Was history repeating itself in her life with the man she had always wanted to trust?

By 1 am, Nisha was thinking how cruel her luck had been. But it was good that she was infected with the Coronavirus. She would soon be free from her 'cursed' life, forever. At least, god would be kind this time by ending her life. She was lost in self-pity; her thoughts turning into a reverie.

She did not quite hear the voice that whispered into her ears; it wafted from another space. She turned and saw Vikram sitting next to her. He was in full PPE kit, but was visibly exhausted. He seemed to be in bad shape.

"What has happened to you?" she asked in fear.

"Nothing. Sorry, I could not come earlier. I was busy arranging a house for us. We cannot stay in your home. We will have to hide in a place where we will not be identified. I have a new SIM card. I have to revisit the plan to escape from here as the 'lockdown' period has been extended." Vikram was in an operation mode.

He explained his plan. She was appalled at first, then wonder-struck. They would break laws. It was a criminal offence for Corona-positive people to hide. The police would search for them. Their phone would be tracked and their relatives would be grilled. During the 'lockdown', people became over-enthusiastic watchdogs, trying to nail the 'breakers of law'.

"Oh! Why do it? After all, dying here is not that bad either."

"No, we are not running away from here to die, but to live. We will live. I am also Corona-positive, I checked on a rapid testing kit. But I am asymptomatic. But I am sure we will survive. Our love will make it happen. You need to be positive about it. Now listen. You will have to change into your doctor's attire, and then walk to the parking lot. We will ride on my bike in full PPE gear so that the police do not stop us. We are going to hide in the Lodhi Estate hostel. It is the nearest 'safe house'

I could manage. We will do it tomorrow noon or night. Tell me what do I have to pack from your home?"

"Can't I go into my own house for some time to take the things out myself?" she asked softly.

"Not, at all. You have to tell me to pack even your petticoats and panties. You can't go anywhere near your home," he replied with the mischievous smile. She looked shy, and blushed like a teenager.

"Then pack things of your choice."

"Yes, I did. And also took some of your artificial jewellery and *bindis* for you, besides the new sets of bras and panties."

He warned her that she had to gather courage, the day after, to go through the physical pain and the stress to put the plan into action. The virus had taken away the last vestiges of her strength.

"I see, this is also one more mission for you. I am happy. You have never failed in your missions. That means we will elope successfully." Nisha's words were tinged with hope – and also sarcasm at the same time.

"Not till we do it actually."

34

22nd April, 2020
29th day of Lockdown

"Why did you tie the hands and feet of that guard and dump him in the washroom? He may not be found out soon, and he will suffer till then," Nisha asked loudly, once inside the car that Vikram had brought to cart her off. She chose not to ask about the car.

"I don't know what will happen to him. But he suspected me and was a danger to us. I could not abandon the plan. It is now or never. I don't think he will die but yes, he will suffer a bit till he is discovered and taken out. There was no way out."

The roads were practically empty, but barricades had been placed at several places. Emergency vehicles appeared suddenly and swiftly.

Nisha did not agree. "No way, I will not live with a murderer. What kind of life I can dream of after depriving another person of his life? Send me back, I will ensure he is well."

Nisha cursed herself for telling Vikram that she wanted to escape. Was he a man or a butcher? Who was this man she loved, a heartless killer?

"Don't be frightened. And stop asking questions. First I will have to dispose this car. I stole it from E Block in Kidwai Nagar three hours ago. The police must be looking for it by now. This vehicle belongs to a senior government officer. It has a MHA pass on its windscreen. It will be easy to move in an official vehicle during the 'lockdown'." He looked at her from the corner of his eyes – waiting for her reaction.

"WHAT? You stole a vehicle. And almost killed a guard. You kidnapped me from the hospital and now you think I will be cool. Are you mad?" She burst out. Anger turned her pale face red, and he could spy repentance, too.

"I would not have stolen the vehicle if the 'lockdown' had ended last week. It is not my fault." He said with an innocent look.

"No, no, it is not your fault, but it is the fault of government which is trying to protect a thief like you, too. Terrible! What nonsense." Nisha was irritated with his skewed logic. She ranted as he drove.

They reached a gated housing complex. The guard at the entrance didn't stop their vehicle on seeing the government pass. He parked near the lift so that they covered the minimum distance possible. He guided her to the lift, carefully.

"Quick, come in and settle down. Keep the door open."

He took her to a room on the fifth floor. He had brought their belongings earlier, along with a stockpile of food for two weeks.

This block of the hostel was built in an asymmetrical hexagonal shape, ensuring maximum privacy to its residents. Many such hostels had been built during the international and national games in the capital city, and thereafter used to house government officials who were waiting for their turn to be allotted homes in their authorised category. These wait-lists often lasted for years.

Soon after seeing her in, Vikram disappeared. When he returned after an hour, he was breathing heavily.

"I had to dump the car in a deserted corner under the Barapullah bridge, quite far from here. Now, we are safe."

He sat down, took a few deep breaths and felt relieved. His mission had been accomplished. He only wished that the security guard of the hospital would not succumb to the injuries he had sustained, when Vikram overpowered him, else it would be quite dangerous for them. He prayed for him quietly.

Nisha was still in shock. What had happened in the last few days was beyond her imagination. She was frightened. And worried about what the world would think about her, and what would be their fate if they were found out. She asked questions, continuously. Vikram would sometimes turn to her and make eye contact or just listen without uttering a word. He knew she would be too exhausted soon to ask anything. She was feeling mildly hysteric. When she fell silent, he fetched her a glass of water, made two cups of tea and sat near her so that they could sip it together.

"Nisha, we are not alone in wanting to disappear like this to live the last few days of our lives as we want. There are plenty like us. Have you read Jonas Jonasson's *The Hundred-Year-Old Man Who Climbed Out the Window and Disappeared*? The main character, Allan Karsson disappeared just before his 100th birthday party, and his escapades were full of adventures and dangerous encounters. The punch line of the book is that you are never too old for an adventure. Similarly, we are never too sick for an adventure. Now chill, and enjoy life."

"Nisha, this house may be where we have to reboot our life into a new one. Let's be positive and move ahead."

It was around 3 pm. He persuaded her to sleep a bit. The 'lockdown' would go on for days in all probability and escapades like theirs would only serve to extend it.

The hostel had one bedroom and one living room, both connected to a washroom. There was a small kitchen near the entrance; it was a self-contained suite. The living room led to a terrace. The rooms had air-conditioning and were furnished. The double bed had a thick mattress and was comfortable. The apartment was airy and they loved to sit with the windows open or in the balcony.

At night, he put the clothes in the *almirah* of the bedroom. He checked the utensils. Fortunately, there were enough. He cleaned them all. He found some jars in the kitchen. He ensured that all the medicines were at an arm's length on a table. He placed the other medical emergency items inside a small cabinet in the living room. He briefed Nisha about the things he was putting in different places so that she would remember where to look for them. They were not sure who would assist whom. The Coronavirus played see-saw with patients. At times, one felt good and then suddenly, one's condition degenerated. The virus was moody – whimsy.

Nisha told him to put two chairs and one small table in the balcony. She wanted to drink her morning and evening tea with Vikram in the little open space, overlooking a clump of green.

They felt relaxed in the new shelter. Vikram picked out a rose from a bouquet in a vase on the table, which he had arranged the day before, and presented it to her; going down on his knees. She giggled and kissed his hand. He felt like her knight in shining armour.

At this moment, this was all the romance they could think of. Thereafter, both of them remained glued to the news on television to know if the police were looking for them and whether the security guard had been rescued. The police had constituted a team to locate Nisha. The guard had been found out and was safe. Vikram was not under suspicion. The army, too, was quiet. There was no news about a Colonel who had deserted his post on the border.

The first day after their escape from the hospital passed mostly in silence, settling down. New and special, though this new togetherness might be, they had to hide from the world. Vikram told her that the apartment had been allotted to an officer, who was transferred to Kashmir later. It was temporarily empty. Then, he briefed her about the security issues. He told her not to switch on her phone's location service or the Internet. In fact, she should not use the gadgets at all. She should not to open the door if anyone knocked. Nisha explained to him about the medicines she was taking, and how to handle the health emergencies arising out of the illness. Vikram was not well, today. Both had fever and body aches.

35

23rd April, 2020

30th day of Lockdown

Nisha woke up early, feeling liberated and elated. She felt better. The morning was pleasant and she could see the sky from the window, which she had missed. The fresh air, natural light and the surrounding trees revitalised her. She wished she could have some fresh flowers, too, but that was not likely. The few plants in the balcony had dried up and flowers were not on sale, these days. A bouquet of roses in the room was fading.

The Coronavirus had levelled everything to the ground. It made her a bit sad but she was determined to work a little to help Vikram as his health had hit a rough patch the night before. He was still sleeping like a log. She waited for him to wake up so that both of them could drink their tea together. Meanwhile, she sipped hot water to soothe her parched and burning throat.

Once Vikram woke up, she poured the tea. Togetherness and tea. His eyes glowed with joy. These were the moments he had dreamt of, for ages. The sunlight that entered the room through the off-white curtains on the windows, dappled like mellow gold. It shone on the love of his life with her cup of tea. They could finally drink their tea together.

"Have a sip and then give it to me, Nisha. It will be sweeter." He extended his cup to her lips.

"My god, you are a die-hard romantic. How did you live alone?"

"Well, I didn't live alone," he replied.

"What?" She was surprised and shocked, she almost shouted at him.

'It was always you. Many a time, I made two cups of tea and sipped both one after another. One in your name." She was placated.

She ordered that they should cook fresh food and keep the ready-to-eat packages for emergencies. They feared that they both could be bed-ridden soon. Vikram said the possibility could not be ruled out; the thought brought a vague unease somewhere at the back of his head. A fear, a strange insecurity.

She cooked rice and a light fish curry for lunch. The fish came from the raw stock that Vikram had sourced from the local market to last for a fortnight. They took more than the usual time to cook, as both of them were slow. They complemented each other in the kitchen, happy. She fed him with her hands. She had always wanted to prepare a dish of fish for him and feed him. He loved the taste of fish, but was scared of the sharp bones, especially the thin, small ones. Vikram reminded her that it was a promise from her days in college she had fulfilled. For the delay in doing so, she would have to pay a penalty. "Leave it, Vikram, we both owe lots of penalties and late fines to each other." Vikram nodded. Sleep suddenly made their eyes heavy – and they drifted off.

In the evening, over cups of hot tea, they filled each other up on their lives. Nisha kept the conversation going. How her life had been in the last 13 years. Her marriage was a mismatch from day one. Deepak did not want to marry her, she was not his first choice but she had no choice after Vikram pulled out. It didn't bother whom she was marrying. However, once married, she wanted to live like a happily-married couple. But fate had different things in store for her.

Deepak was not well-behaved or showed any interest in her. He was ambitious and hard-working. His passion was money. People praised his professionalism but he put a price to everything. She was afraid of his fast-moving pace in life and decided against having children till she understood him well enough. He generally preferred to go to spiffy clubs on holidays and mingle with the 'neo-rich', whereas she loved to stay at home. She felt neglected and dejected, but didn't complain. She accepted that everyone had different perceptions about happiness in life. He was suspicious by nature and accused her of disloyalty to him. He alleged that she still maintained her relationship with Vikram. He nagged her and even turned violent.

Vikram was aghast. "Why didn't you ever protest? You are well-educated, you had financial independence. If you could not raise your voice against the injustice, then who could have?"

He was angry at her, too, for tolerating it. "Couldn't your parents understand this?" he asked her.

"My parents did not have any clue about our trouble because I did not confide in them. They were away. My sister, Neha, you remember – she went to Canada on an assignment. She married a year later and decided to settle down in Canada. My parents also migrated as my father managed to get a job there. Life was better there and they gradually adjusted to the 'foreign' lifestyle. They conveniently forgot me. I didn't feel bad about it. In fact, there was nothing to feel bad about once you disowned me, Vikram. I did not feel bad even when Deepak divorced me after six years. Will you believe that I felt free thinking that if you ever came back, nothing would hold me back from you."

Nisha life's story was long, and Vikram was curious to know the details. But the truth did not feel nice. She had a painful journey, whereas it should have been full of fun.

Many Indians, even if educated, preferred arranged marriages. Few dared to risk marrying of their own choice. They still believed that elders had more wisdom in matters of family and weddings. Nisha was not serious about marriage, and probably let it happen on the rebound. Compatibility factors were not considered.

"Why didn't you turn up ever, Vikram," she asked in a low voice.

"I didn't know about it. In fact, I was jealous of him. So, never felt like finding out."

"I am sure that was not the reason."

"I faced a false rape charge by a Kashmiri girl in 2006 and the case took years to close. She was a girlfriend of a dreaded terrorist called Hafiz. Her name was Noor. Hafiz was involved in several blasts. The order for us was clear that he was to be killed in an encounter. I killed him in an encounter, in front of her. They were planning to marry in a few days and he was visiting her house with bridal gifts and dresses. We had accurate information about the visit. The operation was carried out precisely. He died almost in her arms. She was furious and alleged that I raped her after killing him. The people were biased against us – the security forces – and demanded my head, without any medical report or trial. I was ashamed of this charge."

"Oh! No. But you should have trusted me enough to confide. It was a false allegation. You know me very well and I know you very well, too. You can never hurt anyone."

"Yes, I know but it broke me from inside. I was a captain and had led many operations. I wanted to earn laurels and medals as wedding gifts for you, from my side. So many times, I had put my life in danger to fight the terrorists. And that was what

I got in return. Hafiz had told her that he was a high-ranking army officer in the government of the *jihadi* army and Kashmir would soon be free. He would then be an important person in the government. They could live in Srinagar in a big bungalow. Noor was too young to understand all this. She thought we were the enemy forces, who had occupied Kashmir. She was an orphan and I can understand the emotional influence Hafiz had on her. She was totally in awe of him. It took months for her to realise what Hafiz had been doing." Vikram continued.

"When she understood what had gone wrong, she began to get obsessed with me. It seems a man with a gun always charmed her. She respected an armed man, whether in uniform or not. She started visiting my camp. At first, to buy household goods from my canteen, and then she often wanted to meet me. I was sympathetic to her as I could understand her trauma. I was full of guilt thinking about the families of the terrorists, we killed. Women are the worst sufferers in any conflict scenario."

"Noor wanted me to marry her. But I had no desire to do so. It troubled me a lot. I was already in a mess because of her allegations. I presumed it might be a new ploy by the terrorists to trap us. Around that time, my brother Anurag was also struggling to settle down. The period was crucial. Anyway, I refused to marry her, not once but whenever she asked me to. How can I marry anyone except you? I had a nervous breakdown. When her sister was gang-raped by terrorists and she was molested, she understood the role we soldiers were playing in Kashmir and she withdrew the charge against me. But it was too late. It had damaged me emotionally. After a year, she stopped visiting our camp. Things started falling back to routine at the camp. Once she was out of sight, I started bouncing back."

Vikram's admission came like his redemption, drawing the last of his energy from his body. He was exhausted and wanted a cup of tea. He made two cups of black tea and handed one to her. She was still bewildered by Vikram's story. She did not have any idea what he had to go through, whereas she had been blaming him all these years for deserting her to rise through the ranks in the army. She repented for blaming him.

"Was she beautiful and gorgeous?

"What?" Vikram was taken aback by her query.

"So, she was."

"Maybe, yes."

"Oh! I really feel sorry for you," she sighed.

"Hey, I mean not in that way. I don't judge anyone by their face."

"That's so nice of you. But Noor was beautiful, you remember, don't you?"

"Come on, dear. That was the reason why I kept away from you." Vikram sighed with satisfaction.

"The allegation or Noor?"

"Yes, the allegation."

"So, the allegation was the reason? Hmmm …. Hope, now she had withdrawn her offer of marriage."

"Not exactly," he laughed.

"In fact, I was jealous of your husband and the numerous suitors you had. The fat and chubby guy, the tall and dark professor, and your hospital superintendent, who was so attractive." He said with a smile to lighten the atmosphere.

"Oho, so you know all of them. But you know, you have always been a fool."

She lay back on the bed, tired. She drank hot water and struggled to control her breathlessness. Vikram asked her to close her eyes and rest for a while.

His cough was becoming a major source of irritation, so he though it was wise to rest, too.

They didn't realise when they fell asleep.

36

24th April, 2020

31st day of Lockdown

Around 0430 hrs in the morning, he woke up to the sound of Nisha's heavy breathing. It frightened him. He woke her up and wanted to know what he should do. She asked him to hook her on to the oxygen cylinder. He took it out of the *almirah*, tried to put the mask on her face and open the nozzle of the cylinder. But he was confused. Neither he could fit the mask on her face nor get the cylinder working. She had briefed him about the use of all the medical equipment the evening before, but Vikram hadn't grasped all of it. He was nervous because Nisha was in severe pain. After struggling for a few minutes, he was able to fit the mask properly. And she began to breathe more comfortably.

Vikram cursed himself, he felt clumsy. The medical officers of his unit conducted life-saving courses from time-to-time to make the troops more competent in providing first aid to the needy. He had inaugurated and had been the chief guest in many such programmes, but it had never occurred to him to pick up a few skills.

He had no interest in human anatomy or illnesses. He realised the need to understand the human body clinically, only now. After five hours, Nisha stabilised. By that time, neither had the energy to fetch food from the kitchen to eat. They tried to sleep, praying that they would heal soon. By noon, Nisha was again in pain, while Vikram gathered strength to make tea. They spent most of the day in bed. He felt that she should eat properly to recover. He cooked rice and *dal* - lentil broth - and brought it to her. The simple chore exhausted him so much that he had to sit on a chair and at times, lie on the floor to rest, while cooking. But he did not want his weakness to show.

Vikram slowly fed her with a spoon, her eyes were misty with tears. How loving he was. It must be a dream. She saw his face, noticing the black spot below his eyes. The unshaven beard and the untrimmed moustache could not hide the halo of light, she saw around his head. It made him look so attractive that she was mesmerised. He looked a seer – a *guru*.

Early in the evening, Nisha commented on how blue the sky was. They were sitting in the balcony.

"Yes, it seems bluer than usual, although in Drass I am always in a pollution-free atmosphere. The sky is azure," Vikram said. "But since I am looking at it with you, the sky is a more colourful experience."

The colour of the sky suddenly reminded Vikram of something. He went into the room and came out clutching something in his closed fist. He asked Nisha to hold out her palms. He opened a small bottle of nail polish and started painting the nails of her hands first, and then her legs. A pale shade of shimmering magenta – more pink than purple. She looked at him.

It was the first time he was painting a woman's nails. He spilled colour on the cuticles around her nails. He sat on the floor, while she on a chair. He was trying to do his best, but several times, his hands brushed her skin. These moments were, however, the most precious. After he finished, Vikram sighed with a sense of accomplishment as if he had scaled a mountain. He looked into her eyes expecting a sparkle, but saw that they were moist.

"Why Nisha, have I done something wrong?"

"You have done something I had always longed for," Nisha said softly.

"Is it so? That's good. Then as promised, we will fulfill all our dreams."

"Yes, if we don't die of hunger first!"

That day, she could not count how many times she looked at her nails. She was not only feeling beautiful, but like a princess. The night ended late for them. They spoke about their parents. They were lucky that their parents still remained in good health. Nisha had not informed her parents about her illness.

She had written many letters which they would get if she died. "You have been planning things meticulously these days," Vikram asked.

"Not meticulously, but yes, I am living my own life, good or bad," she replied.

Vikram told her that he had done exactly the same and disclosed everything in letters – and in a 'will', too.

"The Corona has prepared us to die. Had it been thirteen years back, we would have been dreaming of our honeymoon," she said nostalgically. "I wanted to accompany you to Puducherry and be there with you on the beach, but you were so rude." Nisha looked back. She was still hurt.

"Yes, I had been rude to you many times, but now I won't be so. I love you," Vikram said. He could not understand himself, at times. The words echoed in her head. She seemed to have pardoned his absence of the last 13 years.

37

25th April, 2020
32nd day of Lockdown

This morning was not as good as was expected. Due to a rise in positive cases, the 'lockdown' was being seriously implemented. Nisha's condition had worsened. They needed some more medicines and food.

More damaging was the news on the television, showing Nisha's face with the flash that she had been abducted from the isolation ward. An award of INR 1,00,000 had been declared by the police for anyone who could provide clues about her disappearance. The news was circulated, but with a twist. Had it been broadcast as a runaway Corona-positive patient, no one would have probably dared to apprehend her. The police were hoping that she had confined herself to wherever she was. Or maybe, they genuinely suspected that she had been kidnapped as she had always been sincere. The authorities and the police did not expect her to flee the hospital. The search for all the Corona-positive patients, who had fled, had intensified after reports of increasing incidents of infected patients, who were deliberately spreading the virus.

Vikram was prepared to deal with everything. He got up, made tea and *poha* – flattened rice, steamed cooked. Nisha could not move. Her stomach and head ached badly. He brushed her teeth on the bed. She kissed him on the cheeks with toothpaste foam in the shape of her lips. Vikram chided her, as usual, of being too miserly in paying back with a simple kiss. She reached out, held his head with both her hands, pulled him towards her and kissed him passionately.

He wiped her face, made her sit up with the support of the pillows and fed her breakfast. Then, he cleaned the room and the kitchen. Then, he switched on his phone with the new SIM number. He had drawn up a list of home delivery centres, where he made a few calls for medicines and food items. It was not quick service – they had to wait till late in the afternoon for all the orders to be registered.

Life for Vikram was a new roster of duties.

The medicines and the ration would be delivered soon, the shops were trying their best to ensure quick service. The stellar mood of the past few days had waned. The fear of death overshadowed all other concerns in life.

38

26th April, 2020
33rd day of Lockdown

In the morning, after the housework, Vikram sat beside Nisha on the bed. She was struggling to breathe normally. She was still uneasy, but wanted a bath. He had to fix it for her; adjust the right amount of hot and cold water in the faucet. She walked to the bathroom with his help. He stood outside, just out of her view, so that she could wash herself in privacy. But she was too weak to even pour water on herself and too shy to ask Vikram to help. She had never taken off her clothes in front of Vikram – or for that matter for anyone.

After nearly five minutes, when he didn't hear the sound of running water, he wanted to know if everything was okay. In a low voice, she admitted that she was unable to stand on her feet. He found her slumped on a chair, he had placed inside the bathroom. She had not been able to take off her nightdress as she could not raise her hands above her head. He removed it, gently easing the garment off her shoulders. She felt shy, and hid her breasts with her hands. He unhooked the brassiere and handed her a mug of water. Her hands trembled, as she held the mug. He took the mug from her and poured the water, allowing it to slide across her feverish flesh. He soaped her body and then wiped it with a towel, taking care not to hurt her sore flesh. He wrapped the towel around her waist, stripped the panties off her legs as he knew it would be difficult for her to bend down.

He also suggested that she need not wear any undergarments at all. She was shy; and wondered at his wisdom. He took her hand, placed it around his waist and helped her out of the bathroom. He took out a simple dress for her to wear. She first nodded her assent, and then refused asking for a different one – a floral print knee-length cotton frock. Vikram turned to look at her and their eyes met. Both smiled.

"Yes, that's the spirit you need to fight the Coronavirus." He chose one from the cupboard and asked her, "Isn't this the same type that Ivanka Trump wears?" She frowned and retorted, "So, you like Ivanka Trump, not me.

"Put it back and give me my nightie," she was suddenly jealous.

"Oho, come on, *yaar* – pal, I just wanted to know. You will look like a Hollywood actress in this," he laughed.

"No, I won't put it on. I want to look like what I am, and not like any actress about whom you fantasise."

"Nisha, it's not like that. I love you, dearie. I only said it to mean that you are beautiful. The dress suits you."

She didn't say anything, but kept hiding her naked breasts with her hands. Vikram took out another floral yellow print frock from the cupboard. He liked it better than the one she had asked for. He pulled it across her length, drawing the wide cowl -neck down from her head, and smoothening it down her body with his hands. She was happy to see herself in it, like a child. She felt beautiful from inside and wanted him to complement her.

Vikram was observing her silently. After few minutes, he whispered, "You are looking beautiful." He could see her eyes light up. He leaned near her to kiss, she raised her face. He kissed her passionately; the virus was briefly forgotten. The kiss seemed to last for an eternity, dissolving the years, the hurt, the fear of death, anxiety and the disease. The kiss brought them back to life.

They even held each other in the bed, kissing.

Late in the afternoon, they cooked enough food to last for at least four meals. And then went back to bed. Vikram caressed her. This was the way, he had imagined they would be. Inseparable. Forever.

39

27th April, 2020

34th day of Lockdown

They slept till late in the morning. The sun had risen long back, but the rays were soothing. Still sleepy, they reached out for each other across the expanse of the bed and kissed. Vikram pulled her close to him.

After a while Nisha said, "Colonel *Saab*, will you feed me only with kisses or will you give me something to eat?" She had laughter in her voice.

"Oh, you need food, your lips are enough for my breakfast." Vikram was in a naughty mood.

"Get lost! Then what will you ask for lunch?" She pushed him away, lovingly. She was so happy today. He brought her tea and sat next to her, sipping the warm brew. The warmth restored a semblance of energy to his exhausted body. After finishing the tea, he put his head in her lap like a child . She ran her fingers through his hair; rubbed his shoulder and back with her palms. She took a maternal pleasure in trying to lull Vikram to sleep in her lap. He remained still for sometime, remembering his childhood when his mother used to do the same, every time he was tired. Vikram was nostalgic.

Suddenly, he remembered how weak she was. He got up and told her that it was her turn. She happily switched positions and warned him that her turn would be for a longer period. After all, he had denied her this pleasure for too long. The hours passed in laughter and jokes.

In the evening, when he went to the washroom, he realised that his left leg was hurting badly. He was not able to walk straight. He thought it was numbness – loss of blood flow to his limb for sleeping too long in one posture.

He massaged his thigh and calf muscles to increase the circulation of blood to ease the numbness, but the pain increased. He soon sat down holding his leg. The excruciating pain was obvious from his face.

Nisha was worried. "Was there any previous injury?" Vikram was not sure. Then he recalled that just before coming to Delhi he had suffered a minor splinter wound in his leg – the attack and the operations seemed to be distant memories, irrelevant. Nisha examined the leg carefully and found swollen muscles around the wound. The skin had darkened. She suspected that some iron or glass splinters was still embedded in his leg and infected the wound from inside. It needed immediate treatment.

However, she had no surgical instruments here. Neither any medicines. She led him to the bed, forcing him to lie, supine. He had to rest. But the pain did not subside; it soon became unbearable. Vikram writhed with the burning stabs of pain, shooting from his limb, all the way up the spine to his head. She handed him a painkiller, but the impact was short-lived.

The night was hard for both.

40

28th April, 2020

35th day of Lockdown

The infection had probably spread. Vikram soon lost strength to move. Nisha was worried. She asked Vikram if he could arrange for medicines and surgical instruments, as well as a ventilator.

"Are you mad, Nishu! How on earth can I do that? Don't you know I am also a fugitive? Arranging a ventilator is the most difficult thing these days." Vikram was seething in pain. His voice rose by several decibels.

"I see." Nisha was cool and contemplative.

"But why do you need a ventilator? I am okay, except for the infection and the pain," Vikram was genuinely curious.

"It is going to be complicated soon for many reasons."

"How, explain it. Arranging a ventilator is just not possible, I think."

"I know, just think calmly. There must be someone who is resourceful, whom you can trust. Someone, who is as mad as you are."

"What has madness to do here?"

"A lot."

"Like ?"

"He should understand that you have committed *hara-kiri* by coming to me. Then, he should be able to buy or beg or steal these things that we need. And lastly, he should be able to deliver it here."

"Do you think such mad people exist?"

"Yes. One such person is in front of me."

He thought about her suggestion, but could not focus for long. He was running a temperature and was feeling nauseated.

"Vikram, please think, we need all these stuff," she urged him. She held a sheet of paper with the list of medical necessities scribbled on it, but he was not sure who could help. People were afraid to go out of their homes but he decided to take a chance.

He called Puneet Kohli, who was in Dehradun.

"Hi, dummy Colonel, how are you?" Vikram said. His voice sounded shaky and feeble.

"Better than the real Colonel, obviously."

"Tell me, you rascal, are you ready for some adventure?"

"Why not? I can come and kidnap you from your unit in front of your buddies. Tell me."

"Just come and rescue me, and give me some hope to live."

The silence on the other end was eerie. Kohli was shocked at Vikram's plea, he had sounded cheerful barely a week ago.

Kohli had an inkling of serious trouble, he wanted to know what was going on. Vikram handed the phone to Nisha, who updated him about their escape and requested him for the emergency kit, she needed.

Kohli almost burst into tears, but controlled his emotions, answering loudly, "Hold on, bloody Vikram, I am coming to see your ass. Keep yourself alive as I have to kill you with my own hands in the boxing ring. Corona will not have that privilege."

There was a long silence on both sides, no one wanted to hang up. They both were crying, but did not want the other to know.

"Yes, Colonel, I would love to beg anything from you," Vikram said emotionally.

"No, my dear Vikram, you will never beg for anything. Not even to god. I know you both will survive and will make me poorer by a few lakhs as I will have to pay for your honeymoon, which I had promised. I did not know that you were a cheat, *yaar*. I will see you soon." Kohli's genial parting shot brought a faint smile on Vikram's face.

Vikram's condition worsened by the evening. That night was another long one for both of them. She put him on oxygen and forced several pain-killers down his throat. She tried to take the splinter out with a knife after sterilising it but could not succeed. She cut deep gashes, creating fresh wounds and more loss of blood. Now, it was difficult for him to get off the bed. They had to wait for Kohli. It was not an easy task, especially when the borders were sealed and vigilance on movement was tightened. But Kohli was not someone, who could be daunted by challenges and limitations.

41

29th April, 2020
36th day of Lockdown

It was 0830 hours. The weather was cloudy and humid.

Vikram lay helplessly on the bed, while Nisha sat forlorn by his side. They had tea and biscuits, as they waited for Puneet Kohli, who would have to cross three state borders, which were sealed. A ventilator was not easy to carry and if caught, it would be assumed that he had stolen it. Also, it was difficult to arrange for one, for it seemed to be more precious than diamonds now.

Nisha believed in astrology. She checked online for that day's forecast. It was not encouraging.

Around 1100 hrs, Vikram's phone rang. It was Kohli. Without waiting for a hello, Kohli roared, "You bastard, you gave me an address like you had purchased the whole of 'A' block. Tell me the flat number."

"Oh! Sorry, Puneet, we forgot," Nisha responded softly. She requested him to stash the kit at the main gate of the hostel and not to enter the block. But Kohli insisted on meeting Vikram.

Vikram, with Nisha's help, managed to go to the door. He almost crawled to reach it. He could not miss this opportunity to see Kohli. They looked at each other with tears in their eyes, Kohli pleaded with Vikram to let him enter the apartment. Vikram knew him, Kohli was not afraid of dying.

During training, he would go ahead with any dangerous exercise without fear. He didn't know how to swim, but was the first to dive from a height of 35 feet into a pond during the commando jump training to build confidence. Similarly, he was first to bungee jump from cliffs, glide from hills or go rafting in Rishikesh. His favourite punchline was, "I will make fear afraid of me."

Vikram told him to pray for them. Kohli was not sure, but he also knew that Vikram was a man of strong will and would not give up on life so easily.

"Okay, I am going Vikram, but you have to come to meet me with good bottles of Scotch whiskey. You owe me two now. I have brought a few bottles of red wine for both of you. Keep celebrating life. And mind you, if you don't come to me, then you will be a bloody 'Dummy Colonel', not me." Kohli faked a cheerfulness that his face did not show. He spoke shades louder than usual to sound buoyant.

Vikram understood his emotional turbulence, but was too overwhelmed to say anything.

Puneet Kohli went away, unable to bear the sight of his sick buddy. He had travelled through the night by different modes of transport, skipping the police check-posts as well as curfew restrictions. Kohli made it to Delhi on a motorbike criss-crossing village tracks and lesser-known routes, off the highway, to dodge the police.

He had lifted the ventilator from a store of a private hospital, jumped from the building and crept out of the premises like a thief. It was a dangerous escape all the way. Driving bikes on hilly tracks, *kachha* unpaved roads and then on the highways was not an easy task. But Kohli was not meant for easy tasks, either. He was witty, courageous and had a sharp mind. At the same time, he was daring and determined. Once, he had made up his mind to do something, he went ahead with it. Those were the strengths that Vikram depended on, when he called Puneet Kohli for help.

Nisha composed herself after Kohli's emotional departure. He had left an indelible mark on her. Even in such fearful times, he had been a remarkable friend.

Vikram was almost unconscious, drifting in and out of a light coma. She administered him antibiotics intra-venus, and put him on the ventilator. The routine tasks of a doctor made her tired and she collapsed on the bed. She decided to rest for half- an-hour to regain energy. Now, that the emergency supplies were in, she was determined to fight the disease together, howsoever, badly it might have ravaged their systems and bodies.

But she could not wake up, not even in an hour. When she opened her eyes, the clock showed late afternoon. She realised that she had been sleeping or had been unconscious for the last three hours. She remembered Vikram's condition and turned to look at him, next to her. Relief made her light-headed; he was doing fine on the ventilator and the machine was working well. However, Vikram's health parameters were not good. She had to take the splinter out and control the infection before it spread through out his body. The Coronavirus had made it worse. She tried to get up but felt shaky on her legs. She sat back on the bed, took a deep breath to regain her strength. She had to do it now and had to keep moving, somehow. She had to dredge the last of her will power.

After a few unsuccessful attempts to climb off the bed on steady feet, she managed to stand up without support and prepared for the 'treatment'. With a scalpel in hand and everything else that she required, laid out on a table nearby, Nisha created her makeshift operation theatre. She brought water, an energy drink and an oxygen cylinder for herself. She could not afford to be fatigued and swoon during the surgery, leaving Vikram with an open and infected wound, to die.

Then, she paused for a moment to pray to god for the strength and the skill required to cut open the blackened skin on his leg. She whimpered silently, fear numbing for an instant. Instead of touching him with love, she had to cut him up.

For the next hour, she worked on his leg, removing the splinters, cleaning the blood stains, stitching the skin and tending to the wound. He was in pain all the while, and she did not have anesthesia. As he was on a ventilator, reviving him, if he became unconscious again, would not have been possible. She kept speaking to him as she collected the metal and the glass shards, cleaning the open wound with care.

He would not cry in pain to disrupt her. Nothing worked like an ointment to the pain, other than her saying how much she had missed him all these years. An hour later, Nisha relaxed as she bundled the blood stained swabs of cotton into a plastic bin bag. The surgery was a success. She made a cup of tea for herself and sat next to him. His breathing was shallow, but steady. She knew that Vikram would survive. Her professional competence would ensure that he came out a winner.

42

30th April – 2nd May 2020
37th – 39th day of Lockdown

It was already past midnight when she realised that his health was not recovering on expected lines. She was on the edge, but reposed faith in god.

She recalled Vikram telling her, when she was semi-conscious that cuddling helped heal physical wounds faster because of the release of Oxytocin in the brain. Oxytocin was known as the natural 'love hormone'.

She drew him close to her and cuddled him like a child. She felt that she had always wanted to do it, but did not have the courage or the time – or perhaps the right moment – to cradle him. She had dreamed of loving him, kissing him and even sleeping with him. Even under these trying circumstances, she felt the desire rising like a slow spiral of heat in the pit of her stomach. She hugged him sensuously and kissed him, as if he was a pliant toy. Removing the ventilator, she brushed his lips with hers and stared at him, trying to gauge his reaction. It was an act of resuscitation and passion, she could justify her actions as a doctor – and at a deeper level as a passionate human being, who longed to hold him. She saw him moving and responding. In a few minutes, he was breathing normally.

"Hey, you needed love more than medicines," Nisha exclaimed. Vikram smiled and nodded.

Nisha asked him whether he was able to hear her clearly, without strain. "Hmm...," Vikram responded after a few tense seconds. Over the night, he had again slipped into a semi-coma, unable to hear, speak or breathe on his own.

Nisha stretched herself out on the bed and adjusted her position from where they could look at each other and speak. Conversation helped. Oxytocin was also a pain-reliever and a life-saving pill.

She told him that how she had waited for his calls for so many weeks after her wedding, though she knew in her heart that he would not call. After the divorce, she expected him to call, more so, because he had not married and she took it as his love for her. But she was filled with doubts about her self – and her status as a divorcee in a traditional society.

"I knew, you can't marry anyone whom you don't love. And after loving me, you didn't want to love anyone else, isn't it?" It was a pleasant way of reaching out to him and healing him, at the same time. Or perhaps she was reassuring herself with her query – and his response. This had to work.

"Yes, you know me very well. I love you a lot," Vikram murmured feebly. Nisha was more excited to hear Vikram speak; the doctor in her was upbeat at his gradual recovery. The words did not matter much, though the admission of his love for her gave her courage her to dig in, to get a better toehold of the crisis and think of ways to tide over it.

"Love will cure you," she said.

He didn't respond but just kept looking at her. She caressed him and kissed him occasionally, which made both of them smile.

She thanked god for giving her an opportunity to pursue a career in medicine, and the chance to save Vikram's life. She was also happy to have a friend like him, who was ready to do anything for her.

The maternal instinct took over once more. She sang romantic songs from old Hindi movies to make him smile – and then lullabies to put him to sleep. He had no strength to talk; he just nodded at her attempts to cheer him up, helping him get out of the trough he was sinking. She followed the melodies up with a sunny monologue.

"You know, Vikram, beaches have always attracted me. A room in a hotel or a resort with a view of the ocean, a terrace overlooking the sea and a garden on the other side is my dream holiday. I even once wished, if you ever took an early retirement then we could open a 'Book Café n Care' in Goa. You could run the café and book shop, and in one corner I would set up my clinic. The tourist could get medical assistance, drink a cup of coffee and buy a book. I do not need lot of money nor do you, isn't it? We could have had a home on the first floor of the café. And I had thought of a name, too."

Vikram listened attentively and smiled, intermittently. She was revealing her innermost self to him – the romantic carefree soul, the day-dreaming teenager that she really was beneath the dedicated doctor.

At the hint of a name for their dream home, Vikram turned inquisitively towards her. She paused for a long moment as if giving him an opportunity to guess the name – and then said, 'Bohemian Buddha'. The odd pairing of the words got to him. Vikram gave her a 'thumbs up' with a slight twitching of his lips.

This movement was remarkable. While listening to the stories, he was trying to express, move and talk. It was a good sign. His condition was improving.

That day, she was sure there was something more potent a healer than the science of medicines – something unexplained. And that was love.

43

3rd May, 2020

40th day of Lockdown

The morning was bright. The sun touched the tops of the trees with its sparkling rays. Vikram was out of danger, she had managed to save his life. Nisha switched on the television to watch the news.

There was a scoop on a popular news channel, which she often watched. It covered defense-related issues, but with a 'tabloid' twist. The reporter was on location, shouting above the din in the background, "Amidst reports of a border stand-off with China, a colonel in the Indian Army deployed in Drass has fled to save his life. The war in these border areas is imminent or as some say, has already started at a low intensity. In these circumstances, desertion of a unit commanding officer reflects our poor preparedness and impending defeat. This channel has the information about just one officer from our sources. God knows how many more are there. The name and unit of the absconding officer is not known to us so far, but it is believed that the colonel has been compromised by the Chinese, and was being blackmailed."

The channel was good with imagination and fake stories. Especially, against the defence forces. There was not an iota of truth in the story, but a freak incident like this was used to demoralise the troops and Vikram was at the centre of it.

Vikram watched the capsule from the bed. He was still, too, tired to move. The report was damning. And disgraceful, it hurt. The stress began to tell on his physical self. He experienced a sinking feeling inside his heart, and felt breathless. His face paled with the effort to breathe. Nisha switched off the television and strapped the oxygen mask to his face.

She knew the report would hit him and his condition could deteriorate, jeopardising his condition.

44

4th May, 2020
41st day of Lockdown

Nisha removed Vikram from the ventilator after three days. Those three days were the most traumatic for Nisha. Saving Vikram's life was her sole mission, but it also broke her from inside. If he could not cope with the virus, then how would she survive in hiding, alone? She would starve to death. She reacted like a child, but the fact that she was a Corona fugitive and a doctor prevented her from seeking succor anywhere. She could be intercepted and caught – treated like a criminal.

If god had willed death for them, they should die together. Her thoughts swung in random arcs these days. She hardly slept and was engrossed in tending to Vikram. It taxed her Covid-riddled system. When he began to gain health, Nisha weakened. The virus was still incubating. It seemed that the cosmos was maintaining a balance of life between them. Maybe, only one of them was destined to live, love had compelled *Yamaraj* – the god of death – to choose between them. She told Vikram that she had been stealing his life. She was supposed to die and her life had no meaning after her failed marriage and the Covid-19 infection.

Vikram said that his life should end as he had earned all the laurels he wanted to, the rolls of honour he aspired to, but not love. Once, he had seen love in her eyes, his life was full. She had endured pain and deprivation, thus she had to live to experience life's pleasures, too.

"Your infinite love for me has made you my absolute happiness. Life has no meaning, once you have experienced these feelings," Nisha replied emotionally.

"Hey, don't worry, I am yours forever."

"Yes, mine and mine, only."

"Aren't you a bit greedy?"

"What do you mean by greedy? Do you want to belong to someone else, too?" She pretended to be angry with him and turned the other way.

"Oh ho! So, now, my queen needs a bit of love. How did you live so many years without me?"

"I didn't live, I just breathed. You know, Deepak never even touched me or cuddled me with tenderness. For him, my body was just a tool of sexual pleasure. There was nothing for me, there. The marriage was always agonising for me physically and emotionally."

Her words dulled the intimacy of the moment. Vikram knew he was responsible for her torture at the hands of her husband, he was guilty. Had he been there, their lives would have been different. Their break-up had shattered Nisha, whereas he had used it to divert his energies to pursue success in his career and reap the rewards.

45

5h May, 2020

42nd day of Lockdown

The morning brought disturbing news.

The hospital guard whom Vikram had tied up and abandoned in the washroom had tested positive for Corona. A television report said the person who had immobilised him was responsible for the infection and should be charged under the Epidemic Act, too. No one was sparing any opportunity to link law and order incidents to the Corona pandemic. She calculated the days. The incident took place on April 22, thus it was with in the isolation period of 14 days.

It dampened their spirits. More so Nisha's, who again lapsed into a repentance mode for agreeing to flee with him.

46

11th May, 2020

48th day of Lockdown

The last few days had been agonising. The few survival stories of the Corona patients were their only hope. The stories gave them strength. At other times, the fear of death took away the positivity. They plunged into bleak despair.

They knew that no one could love each other as much as they did. And if love was the only therapy, then probably, they had overcome this illness.

While listening to one such survival story, Nisha kissed him passionately. Nisha always said that 'these lips were her lifeline'. Till the time, she had 'this medicine, she would be fighting-fit like the valiant Colonel'. She was feeling loved, and found herself aroused. She not only kissed his lips, but kissed his chest, too. For a moment, they forgot that they were seriously ill. He felt aroused, too. It was surprising, how could it be?

How could two fragile bodies, surviving on artificial support, have so much energy? He thought this eroticism was in his mind, their bodies could not support the passion. But they were wrong. A languor gripped them as their caresses became more intense. Nisha clung to Vikram, the clothes felt like a barrier between them. They removed the layers of fabric that seemed to envelope their flesh to feel the freedom of their overwhelming love. They had never seen each other in the nude – stark naked. It was a revelation. Both kept looking at each other for quite some time. They were not sure whether they could make love to each other, but felt better as they climaxed.

The act of lovemaking exhausted them, sapping the last of their energy. They lay spent, staring at the ceiling. The dappled sunlight cast strange shapes on the whitewashed space.

They did not realise when they fell asleep. When she woke up around six in the evening, she saw Vikram sizing her up like an exhibit, from the top to the bottom.

She felt shy. She wanted to know if he had ever seen a naked woman.

"No never, not from so near, a real one."

"I can't believe it," she said dismissing his reply.

"Why do you want to know?"

"Means, you have seen. Who was she?" Stabs of jealousy made her fume. Vikram laughed at her possessiveness. "No one, *yaar*, but used to watch pornography sometimes, that's all. I always dreamt of you." Nisha was still unbelieving. He was too good to be true.

She got up to cook dinner. Vikram followed her. The bonhomie that bound them in the bed spread to the kitchen, as well. They worked together on the chopping board and over the oven. It had been three days since they had eaten. Both were hungry. And they gorged on the frugal fare like children.

Later, she took out some chocolates from the fridge and shared them with Vikram.

The plus point was that their metabolism seemed to be working well. Immediately, after dinner, they feel asleep.

47

12th May, 2020
49th day of Lockdown

Next morning, they woke up around 9 am.

The memories of the previous day were still fresh, lingering in their tenderness and in embers of unbridled desire. After tea, their eyes met with naughty laughter. They hugged each other spontaneously, kissed and cuddled again. Intoxicated, they stole soft moments of love whenever their dissipated energies would permit. Corona had acted as a Cupid for them, it seemed.

After a short nap, Vikram sprung a surprise on Nisha. He took out a red-and-white *Bengali sari* – the traditional Indian drape woven in Bengal – and artificial jewellery. He told Nisha to dress like a bride. He wore a light blue *kurta* – the long Indian shirt – and a white *pyjama* – loose traditional pants . He wanted them to marry right then, right there.

She agreed. She draped the *sari* and tried her best to put on make-up on her face. Vikram suggested that she wear a big red *bindi* – brow dot – and red lipstick. She had a broad forehead, a big sharp nose and heart-shaped lips. Her looks still stunned

Vikram. To him, she looked like an Indian goddess in the *sari*. He kept gazing at her.

Something was amiss. He realised that she needed some flowers to weave around her hair or a wreath around the neck to make the ensemble perfect. He asked her to wait. He put on the face mask and sprinted out. He wanted to pick flowers from the gardens in the neighbourhood.

He remembered seeing flowering shrubs nearby, while coming back after disposing the stolen car. They were mostly wall flowers – creeping and blooming amidst the ivies, delicately coloured, around walls and the hedges. He was back in an hour, with a handful of them. He put the jasmine blossoms and a rose that he stole from the garden next door in her hair. He also threw some of the rose petals on the bed and joked, "See our honeymoon bed is ready, too."

She replied seriously, "Yes, it is an essential ritual."

They married each other in the name of god.

Finally, they were husband and wife. Vikram was floating on a cloud. She was his, forever. Oh! it was such a nice feeling. He could have had this wonderful moment 13 years ago.

Now, those lost years had to be lived in the next few days.

48

18th May, 2020
55th day of Lockdown

A rainbow cloud of happiness hung in their hostel room. Vikram and Nisha were full of joy. Their health had started improving. They were still weak but their immune systems were working. They were eating more. She cooked French fries in the evening. Vikram remembered that Kohli had brought them some bottles of wine, which they drank together though they were not sure whether they would be able to digest the beverage due to their illness.

Nisha was a teetotaller.

Vikram called Kohli and told him about their wedding. Kohli was now sure they would survive. He had been worried about them after returning from Delhi.

Today, 'Lockdown 3.0' was to be called off. It had been more than 21 days they were unwell. In all probability, the worst was over. But the pandemic had been spreading and the situation in Maharashtra was beyond control. Delhi was still within bounds.

Labourers were migrating from Maharashtra, ferrying the virus with them wherever they went. 'Lockdown 4' was announced. However, many exemptions were allowed, and it was not likely to impact their lives much.

That night Vikram lit a candle, opened a bottle of wine and poured it in two glasses. It was the best he could do to recreate a romantic candlelight dinner date. Both couldn't stop smiling. They finished the bottle of wine over the next two hours – recalling the best of their dreams, which were slowly becoming real.

The wine carried them to a new high, taking away the fear and the chaos they had endured for the last four weeks. She was attired in a long frock. He wore a light blue shirt with full sleeves, black trousers and a festive necktie. Once the 'lockdown' was over, they planned a holiday in Goa.

That romantic mood continued late into the night. They called it their wedding night. They were now hopeful of surviving the Coronavirus.

They went to sleep well after midnight. They wanted to take a stroll, once the extended 'lockdown' was over in the next few days – probably to walk away to freedom. They decided to go for a Coronavirus test, the day after. They were also planning their future.

The last four weeks had been an odyssey of discovery for them. Love was the biggest immunity booster against the virus, and if dished out in plenty, it could tackle any disease.

49

21st May, 2020

58th day of Lockdown

They tested themselves in the morning. The report was negative.

News about the Corona patients surviving were pouring in from many places. Though in India, the infections were rising daily in record numbers, elsewhere around the world, the recovery rate was offering slivers of hope. A vaccine was the demand of the day. Nisha said that she would offer herself to any such experiment.

"That may be dangerous and could affect your health and life," Vikram said apprehensively.

"Yes, it can."

"So, why to take the risk?" Vikram asked.

"I am just as passionate about my profession as you are about yours."

They received a shock while watching the news on the television. "Businessman arrested for stealing ventilator in Dehradun." It was Kohli. He had been arrested for the theft and was accused of violating 'lockdown' norms. The ventilator had been stolen from a private hospital and they had tracked it to him.

Kohli was not aware that data about the movement of essential commodities were compiled and corroborated. There was no record of any sale of ventilator and on the contrary, there was a report of a theft of one. The Kohlis were respected in the city and the arrest was a fall from grace. A family known for charity and donations had been caught stealing.

The police were interested in knowing the motive behind the theft.

•

50

24th May, 2020

61st day of Lockdown

It was a pleasant Sunday morning. The weather was still kind to Delhiites though the occasional 'earthquakes' were scary. They were still asleep, when the doorbell rang. They wondered who could be at the door during the 'lockdown' on a Sunday. They were not expecting any one.

Vikram reluctantly got up and headed for the door. Still sleepy, he put on his face mask first, then urinated. The ringing stopped. He took off the mask, and went back to sleep. No sooner he had reached the bedroom, than the bell rang again. He put on the mask and opened the door, this time.

The colour drained from his face at the sight of the small posse at the door. The military police and the Delhi police had located them. The captain in charge of the team said, "Sir, you are under arrest. And Dr. Nisha, you, too."

"Yes, I can see that. But how did you find us?" he asked.

The captain continued. "Since you both are suffering from the Coronavirus, we are locking you here. A guard will be posted outside. Here are some test kits. When both of you test negative twice, let us know."

He pushed the test kits and then, handed a small packet of groceries and chocolates with a card addressed to Vikram through the narrow gap in the door that was still barred by the safety-latch chain. The captain said that he respected Vikram for what he had done, but for breaking the army rules, he would need to arrest the Colonel; probably for a court martial.

Vikram returned to the bedroom. Nisha overheard the conversation. She said she would prefer to die here than rot in jail after the last four 'traumatic' weeks . Or, why not flee again. May be that way, they would be able to live the way they dreamt of and then court death.

Vikram assured her that nothing much would happen. Her crime was not serious, and secondly, he would say that he had forcibly kidnapped her. And as far as his crime was concerned, an army court would consider his case. He told her that considering his achievements, they would take a lenient view and the maximum punishment could be removal from the services, possibly a short stint in jail. They could easily lead a happy life, thereafter. They smiled, though they were worried.

Till a few days ago, they were not even worried about their 'impending death' from the Coronavirus, but now they feared a few months of imprisonment. They lived for each other now, love had breached their armours of brash courage. Earthly emotions like possessiveness, jealousy and pleasure dominated their minds.

Vikram said 'whatever happens, let it happen. They should not stop loving each other.' It was as if they had been suddenly thrown from a lofty perch of ideals they had been inhabiting to the hard ground of reality, below. They were mere humans, puny in their fears.

That day, they both tested negative. They tested themselves as directed by the team, who came to arrest them. Therefore, in all probability, they were free of the Coronavirus, but the house was not virus-free. This test could not guarantee that they were virus-free as one more test had to be conducted after a day or two.

The accuracy of the rapid test kits was also questionable. It was widely rumoured that China was sending sub-standard testing kits all over the world. Many countries were returning them. The Indian Council of Medical Research, too, had withdrawn certain categories of testing kits.

Nevertheless, it was great news for them for the simple reason that they were out of danger. The critical phase of the illness was over. They had come out alive. When they fled from the hospital, they had been ready to die together. They celebrated their test reports by cooking together. The team deployed to confine them had brought fresh vegetables – an exceptional pleasure in these 'withering' times.

After cooking, Vikram suggested that they shower together, striking off one more 'must-do' from their wish-list. Soon, their bodies were glowing in the warm fragrance of love.

Quarantine also brought joy.

51

25th May, 2020
62nd day of Lockdown

Today, they conducted another test, which was also negative. It was a relief.

The 'lockdown' had been partially relaxed. The virus had left behind a debris of destruction and waste in its insane run. People were talking about the plight of the migrant labourers, who tried to hurry home to escape the scourge.

In the intense April heat, they were dying on the roads while cycling or walking, in vehicle accidents, on platforms at railway stations waiting for trains – and inside the trains while returning to their home towns. The Corona was just unfolding in its nightmarish first act. It was happening due to the insensitivity of the people, the officials and the politicians, Vikram felt that a sincere will to leash the virus was missing.

The military police took Vikram away, while Nisha was handed over to the Delhi police. She was produced in court on the same day.

Her plea was that she had not spread the disease nor it was her intention because she was dying. She wanted to go into hiding with her lover to live her last moments in contentment and happiness. Since she was diagnosed with the virus, she had relapsed thrice. The chances of survival of patients hit by the Coronavirus thrice were not good. Thinking that her death was imminent, she fled the hospital and hid in a hostel, but in quarantine.

Nisha put on her best lawyer's 'robes' in the court, arguing from a high moral ground to earn sympathy from the arbiters – and a bail. The judge didn't see any criminal intention on her part, and sympathising with her services to her patients, took a lenient view. She was granted bail. There was nothing much to investigate. The police didn't oppose her plea for bail. There was no use in increasing the numbers of prisoners during the pandemic. The jail authorities were releasing prisoners who were charged with minor offenses, and the police were taking very few into custody.

By evening, she was back to the hospital guest house. Her home had to be sanitised before she was allowed to move in. The hospital administration had suspended her services till the completion of a formal inquiry. She was not interested to continue her job at the hospital. Her sole interest was Vikram and she wondered how she could meet him again. To reconnect and reunite. She did not intend to lose the threads, she had picked up after 13 years.

Vikram was to be taken to Udhampur at the Corps headquarters, a nearly 12-hour journey by road.

52

26th May, 2020
63rd day of Lockdown

The Colonel was taken to the Corps HQ in an army vehicle. The olive-green Bolero reminded Vikram of his motorcycle journey, his reckless ride through the rough terrain of the Himalayas, almost a month ago. That was thrilling, unlike this one. Now he was under arrest, being led to an army court. An officer whose stories of bravery were once cited as 'examples' would be disrobed of his honours, soon. He wished for death than this dishonour.

They reached their destination in Udhampur after a gruelling 12-hour drive. Families of the army *jawans* and the officers alike flocked to see him when he reached the campus. They were curious. It is said in the army, 'you get your battalion first, then your wife.' So, your first duty is towards the battalion. But Vikram had prioritised the latter.

His trial would take place there – on the campus.

The corps and the regiment, which till recently congratulated him on his successes, would soon be hearing of his 'offenses'.

The Chief of Army had ordered a swift court martial. Any delay would only bring adverse publicity. His court martial would begin next Monday, after six days. He was in custody, confined to a room in the annexe of the officers' mess.

Charges had been framed against him. The convening authority had given him the papers and directed him to defend his case. He could seek help from any serving or retired army man or his family member to defend his case.

To argue his case, he wanted to consult Kohli. Yesterday, Kohli had been released on bail. The hospital had requested the court to permit them to withdraw the theft report. Because of his family's history of philanthropy, the public sentiment went against any kind of prosecution.

Vikram thought Kohli should plead his case but later, decided to do it himself. A person released on bail a few days ago should not be pleading his case. But, he wished Nisha was present at the hearings. Her presence would give him strength. But, it might not be prudent. He was a disgraced officer who would be 'named and shamed'.

Late in the evening, Nisha and Kohli called to say that they would be coming to Udhampur. He wanted to stop them, but they refused to listen to him .

He was afraid that Kohli would be mocked, further. Vikram did not want the HQ to poke fun at Kohli. People could say that it was good that a thief like Kohli had left the army early. Vikram was ambiguous about their presence at the court martial.

53

27th May, 2020

64th day of Lockdown

Amid all this, Vikram arranged to send his parents away for a few weeks to an *ashram* – spiritual retreat – near his native place where they wanted to go for a long time. They did not know what was happening, Vikram ensured that they were kept out of his controversial arrest– and any blitz surrounding it. In the battalion, they had been taken care of even after Vikram's desertion.

Defending oneself in a court martial was not an easy task. That, too, when he could not deny the facts. Objections would be in the interpretation of the exigencies and insufficiency of evidence. The view which he could take would be a head-on collision with the prosecution's charge.

Nisha and Kohli reached Udhampur late in the evening. They stayed in a hotel as Nisha was denied accommodation in an army officer's mess because she was not from an army background. Kohli preferred to stay in the hotel, too. He didn't want to leave her alone. He felt a fierce moral indignation against the attitude of the army towards Nisha. He was contemptuous about conventional respectability. He firmly believed that love was worth any cost, you could not put a tag or riders to it.

However, this was just the first in the series of humiliations which were to follow.

54

29th May, 2020
66th day of Lockdown

The court was convened to serve charges on the officer before the start of the examination of witnesses. The Colonel had been issued a notice, the day before, with a memorandum of charges.

The prosecuting officer, Judge-Advocate Colonel Sanjeev Mahapatra sought the permission of the presiding judge or Judge-Attorney Brigadier Kumudini Patel – to add a few more charges before the proceedings began. He pleaded that the convening authority had missed the disciplinary aspects and had not paid adequate attention to other details. He added that Colonel Vikram had not only committed an offence 'unbecoming of an officer' by deserting unit command, but some more offenses, as well.

Mahapatra read the charges. "Whereas, he had committed a heinous offence by deserting the unit during an active operation; he had committed the heinous crime of deserting, an action which was of immediate gain to the enemies. Thus, it was an act of treachery and cowardice."

"Whereas, the Colonel had left his troops leaderless during a crisis without any lawful authority, was not just misconduct of 'unbecoming of officer' but running away from war, which is an act of treason towards the nation, shall be punishable in the eyes of law."

"Colonel Vikram has broken the rules of the 'lockdown', a violation of instructions and curfew regulations, punishable offence under Section 2 of the Epidemic Disease Act."

"Colonel Vikram kidnapped Dr. Nisha from the hospital by incapacitating a guard and enticing her on the false promise of treating her well. A despicable criminal offence."

"Colonel Vikram sought help from a friend to get the hostel accommodation by hiding the fact that he was suffering from Covid-19, thus a breach of trust, which is not befitting in the manner of an army officer and thus guilty of violation of army's code of conduct.

"Colonel has stayed with a lady, like husband and wife whereas they were not married. This is an act of moral turpitude."

The prosecutor pleaded with the judges that these offenses needed exemplary punishment of imprisonment and not merely dismissal from service.

The Judge Attorney, as per rules, asked Colonel Vikram to seek time to respond to the charges and could engage any officer as a defense counsel, if he wished to.

Vikram said that he didn't need any time to defend himself and would be arguing his own case. Rather he prayed to the court that the proceeding be completed as soon as possible. Upon this, the prosecutor mocked him, saying that Vikram was in a hurry to sleep with Dr. Nisha and wanted a General Court Martial procedure to be over in a day.

The judge attorney rebuked the prosecutor and told him to be careful in the use of his words and personal attacks, not concerning the case.

Kumudini Patel, an officer who had fought for equality of opportunity for women, was the first woman in the army who had risen to this position. She was known as a no-nonsense officer, highly professional and courageous. She had faced discrimination in the army due to her gender and was therefore determined to prove that even as part of combat troops, women were among the best. She had earned a gallantry medal for killing two terrorists in Kupwara sector, when she was a captain in the Rashtriya Rifles. No doubt, she was the right person to preside over to such a unique and high-profile case.

She ordered the court to convene the next day and asked both the parties to be ready to deal with the case expeditiously.

55

30th May, 2020
67th day of Lockdown

The session resumed next morning. Vikram sought the permission of the Judge-Attorney to counter the perception of the prosecution on the charges levelled against him.

First, he took up the matter of demeaning Nisha, taking offence to Colonel Mahapatra being disrespectful. He demanded that the prosecutor address Nisha with respect. He requested the judge that the army administration allow her to stay with him. He reminded the court that he was still not proven guilty of any offence and his apprehension from Delhi was just to ensure his presence in court. He was still a decorated officer, who had brought laurels to the regiment.

Colonel Sanjeev countered, "He may have high regard for women, but by merely sleeping with someone doesn't make her his wife. Colonel Vikram must be aware of the rules which define who are husband and wife. This attitude that he is above the law is the major problem with the Colonel."

Vikram informed the court that they had married when they were in isolation and had clicked a few pictures on the phone. On being asked for proof and witnesses or certificate, he said that there were no witnesses. "The solemnisation of a marriage of two souls doesn't require any witnesses. The union of two willing persons doesn't wait for any certification."

He also pleaded that the prosecution could keep raking up such defamatory charges and allegations, so it would be prudent to decide the case as soon as possible. He reminded the court that he had been awarded five gallantry medals, including a *Shaurya Chakra* and two wound medals. His credentials were far above any serving officer and his leaving the unit was not an act of cowardice. It was for a noble cause.

Vikram pleaded with the court to direct the prosecution to address Nisha with respect as she was his wife.

The prosecutor said that he would definitely be respectful to her but could not recognise her as the wife of the Colonel.

Vikram objected.

"That is the problem with the Colonel, my honour. He thinks whatever he does is the law. The marriage has to be solemnised/registered with the authorities or sanctioned in court. He did neither. He thinks we should accept whatever he says."

"Sir, we married in a different situation. It was our dying wish. I request the court to ascertain from Nisha and confirm our marriage. As Coronavirus-positive patients, we could not have done anything else. In Hindu scriptures, this has sanctity."

Nisha was in tears listening to the arguments about the authenticity of her marriage. She thought that she was in a man's world, more so in the army. Do army folks still subscribe to the myth about inferiority of women? It is born out of attitude. Her 'attitude' should also decide who was stronger. She wanted to speak out and snub the prosecutor.

The judges didn't think this issue required much deliberation. Registration of the marriage, as per law, was not possible when it happened. He said it was a marriage between two consenting adults and a rather humane gesture when death was imminent.

"I appreciate the commitment of Colonel Vikram and recognise them as a married couple. Dr. Nisha is now wife of an army man." Looking at her, the presiding judge said, "Welcome to the army family."

Then, he looked at the bench where prosecuting team was sitting and said, "We honour this marriage and the dignity of the lady. We also appreciate the Colonel. Hope the matter ends here."

Colonel Vikram again requested the bench to expedite the process and arrive at a decision soon to avoid media glare.

The presiding judge asked for a recess of 15 minutes to consult the other judges and the prosecution. In times such as these, it was best not to prolong contentious issues. It was critical, too, as Pakistan had been continuously violating the cease-fire on the border. Also, India had stopped the Chinese takeover of Indian companies and the Chinese government was in an aggressive mode on the border.

The court martial of a decorated officer, who had deserted the unit could have wider implications and therefore needed to be decided as soon as possible. In response to his written submission, Vikram had confessed to have left the unit on his own after 'leave was denied to him'.

The judges unanimously decided not to adjourn the court till the case was decided on Monday. When it reassembled after a solemn weekend, both the prosecution and the defense were ready to cooperate. The Army HQ had indicated that the trial should be low-profile.

After the court was adjourned, Vikram met Kohli and Nisha. He hugged both of them.

"Thanks a bunch for making it here," Vikram said to Kohli in a low voice. Kohli whispered to him that Vikram should not ask him to speak in his defense as he could end up abusing many colonels and generals.

"You know how stupid they are in my opinion." He told Vikram to be passionate and firm in his argument. The Army is all about being truthful and being a gentleman, forever.

"Yes Kohli, but I deserted the unit. And that is an offence." Vikram was not sure how to defend the desertion charge.

"Vikram, you have to defend it. You can't go to jail. Now, Nisha is in your life and she cannot be left alone."

"I don't want to but …"

Kohli set forth the line of argument. "You didn't desert the unit. You were denied leave. You requested it, repeatedly. The army could have made arrangements for your replacement. No one is indispensable in any system. They were autocratic in their approach by denying you leave, compelling you to proceed without permission. When it is question of love and war, everything is fair."

Kohli's message was clear: Tear apart the Brigadier and the General, who refused the leave, vilify their colonial mindset. Accuse them of bias. Berate their so-called professional judgment which is obviously biased.

56

1st June, 2020

69th day of Lockdown

The court assembled at 0930. The presiding judge, Brigadier Kumudini Patel, pronounced that the court would not adjourn till the proceedings were over.

It would grant recess for consultations and meals.

Neither the prosecution nor the defense should try to prolong on any pretext. And till the decision was made, nobody would be permitted to move out of court premises or pass information to anyone outside. The proceedings were to be held *in camera* and any witnesses, if needed, would be called on video conference.

This arrangement was unique for a court martial. But times had changed since the pandemic began. During the 'lockdown', cases were argued from jails and judges dispensed justice from their homes. There was wider acceptance of these processes. Obviously, the time had come to change the way justice was being administered. However, the armed forces were always the last to change. They preferred to stick to traditions.

The prosecutor pressed his charges, saying, "The act of Colonel was one of gross indiscipline, insubordination and cowardice. He had shamefully abandoned the unit from a forward post when it was under attack. It was an act of treason."

The Colonel refuted the charges saying he had not abandoned the post. He had requested his Brigade commander and GOC to grant leave, explaining the situation and pleading repeatedly. But they failed to appreciate the urgency. It was surprising that they did not trust him.

"But we all know leave cannot be claimed as a matter of right by any army man. If during war, all want to go on leave, then what would happen," the prosecutor countered.

"Yes, but certain situations in one's life can be different and at that time, compassion should prevail. After all, wars cannot be decided in a day nor can a soldier's loyalty be tested from one odd incident."

"So, if you are not granted leave, then you will desert your men like this."

"I had made proper handing-over instructions to the officer, next in command."

"Who was that?" asked Major Sanjeev Mahapatra.

"My Adjutant Major Gogai."

"And who is next to you in seniority in unit."

"Lt. Colonel Rawat. But he was injured five days ago in action and was shifted to base hospital in Srinagar for treatment."

"My honour, the second in the chain of command was indisposed and that, too, in action. You can well imagine how volatile the situation was for the unit. Still, the Colonel in all his wisdom chose to hand over charge to a Major-rank officer, who had not yet been groomed to take over the battalion."

"I had spoken to the brigadier and GOC and requested them to make arrangements, but they rebuffed my requests. I had no other option." Colonel replied.

"Okay Colonel, you have been commanding battalion and when your Major is on leave and your captain is injured, to whom do you assign the charge of that company."

"I would assign it to some other Major or Captain from Unit HQ or other companies."

"Exactly, that is the standard protocol. But the Colonel in his wisdom didn't follow this. May I know the reason behind it?"

Vikram was hung by his own logic. Commanding a battalion was a serious issue, especially when it was deployed at a forward post and was under attack from enemies. Can a junior officer be competent enough to appreciate the situation and take bold decisions?

"My case was different. Nisha was seriously ill and I thought I must go there immediately to help her."

"What kind of help could you render? Are you a doctor? Did you have a panacea for the Coronavirus?" The prosecutor was obviously not convinced of the urgency.

"No, I am not a doctor. But you will appreciate, when you are seriously ill and suffering from a life threatening disease, you want someone to take care of you."

"Yes, I will desire so Sir, but the Coronavirus is not a disease where you are allowed to do so. And why call it life-threatening when the mortality rate is less than 5% and in India, it is less than 3%, so far."

"I agree, but you can't rule out the importance of love and care, which plays a vital role in enhancing the immunity of patients in coping with diseases."

"My lord, the Colonel, after earning his medals, has bestowed upon himself the status of god. He thinks that his touch will work magic and the patient will come out like a superman. I think, he has been irresponsible in his conduct. How can we trust him with the job of commanding a unit? He may go to Pakistan or China to meet the enemies and befriend them, rather than responding to their attacks."

Asking the Colonel to counter his argument, he said everyone was aware that Corona patients were quarantined in isolation wards and no one was allowed to go near them except for the health-workers in full protective gear.

"Sir, I agree that nobody is allowed. But I was ready to die with her. I missed marrying her 13 years back. All these years, I earned my respect, medals and honours but there was something amiss in my life. The moment I realised it was her, I wanted to spend time with her."

"Colonel, and you risked your life for this."

"Yes, it was not the first time I risked my life. The army loved me whenever I took such risks. The medals and the appreciation are examples of that love."

"Yes Colonel, that was for a cause. That was for the country."

"Yes, one needs to take risks in life, only then can they can do so for the country."

"How can you equate your beloved with your country? Your duty comes first."

"I am a human being and humanity comes first."

"Doesn't this humanity teach you to protect your troops, after all, so many lives have been at stake."

"I didn't leave them in a lurch, the whole set-up was there and they were in able hands. My officers have been groomed to take up challenges."

"And you think that doctors of a prestigious hospital like Safdarjung are not groomed to take care of patients that you had to go to take care of one." The prosecution nailed him.

Vikram was silent.

Kohli indicated to Vikram to seek a recess. It was 1430 hrs. The judge granted an hour's recess for lunch.

During the break, Kohli asked, "Are you serious about defending yourself?" Vikram did not answer him.

Kohli said Vikram was not leading the argument in the right direction. He was getting trapped in the version which the prosecution wanted from him. He needed to focus why humans needed love to sustain life. It was love and passion which protected a nation, and this love came from individual transactions, first.

What is a country? Isn't it an entity which army personnel are told to love? Isn't this required of all countrymen? Then, how could it be unequal for citizens. It is so because of the sense of duty? Another dilemma – which duty first? Towards human beings or the country, first. Isn't it a fact that a country consists of human beings?

Nisha was very tense. She could not eat anything. When Kohli insisted, she spooned some salad and rice with *dal* – lentil broth — on her plate, but left most of it untouched!

Incidentally, everyone – the judges, prosecution and the defense were eating together in the same hall. The prosecution team was wary. In uniformed services, everyone wanted to succeed. Defeat was the word that pinched hard.

The line of argument had to be deviated from processes and procedures as it would go against the Colonel. Vikram had to focus on the fact that he tried to follow all the existing procedures and his requests of leave was denied without taking into consideration his reasons.

He had to blame his bosses for being callous in spite of his excellent track record. He had to put his major-general's wisdom in question. He had to tell that the general failed miserably in appreciating this issue. The Colonel didn't want to blame anyone for what he did. And he didn't think that they had done any injustice to him because at such a critical time, it was the best decision to keep an officer of his calibre at the post.

Kohli had a tough time convincing Vikram that he was not suggesting any kind of 'mudslinging or rebellion'. Vikram would just challenge their administrative decisions. Such challenges were not only without malice, but the right of every serviceman as a grievance-redress mechanism. At the same time, no specific reason was given about the denial of leave.

"Leave or any requests are denied like this with just a one-line missive, 'due to Ops and Adm exigencies' the competent authority has refused the prayer of the officer," Colonel Vikram told Kohli.

"Yes, I know and that's why I am saying so. It makes the situation at the forward post a normal one and thus under such circumstances, your leave should not have been denied."

It was difficult for Kohli to make Vikram understand that he had committed the mistake of 'absence without leave' and not deserted the unit. Desertion is the intention to run away from the army and not to return ever. Vikram did not have any such intention nor he was afraid of taking on any challenges.

Kohli collected data from various forward posts. The Drass camp faced 50-80 skirmishes every year, literally more than one every week. That didn't mean that no one from the camp would be allowed leave.

Kohli listed the points for Vikram. They discussed the distances from his unit to other bases, from where any other Colonel could have replaced him within a few hours. He had also arranged for the helicopter which took off from the area on the fateful day, the Colonel decided to leave the camp. Kohli also convinced him that no other charges were tenable. Going to take care of a patient during 'lockdown', who was alone and helpless could not be a sin, but just violation of instructions in spirit.

"You have got a point, Kohli. I will take care of it."

Kohli sighed, and wished him best of luck with a pat on his back.

Vikram had been a debater from his days in college, cool and composed in his arguments.

His responses used to be precise. He did not indulge in a heated exchanges or hammer his opponent. After listening to his opponents, he would demolish their views with powerful logic. He understood the amazing power of words which came to him naturally.

Colonel Vikram then rose for his final submission. He turned his head to look at Kohli and Nisha, sitting in a corner. Nisha's eyes were moist. There were signs of unease on her face. When her eyes met with his, she seemed to be saying, 'Just come out of it, I have got my liveliness back after ages and don't want to be just a breathing corpse again.' When Vikram saw the tears in her eyes, he resolved to change his approach. The army had to start respecting and prioritising human values. He felt that her prayers were giving him strength.

All eyes were fixed on the Colonel. He threw a cursory look at the prosecution team and then turned to the judges.

A large number of officers had assembled in the courtroom as the trial was an instant hit. It was almost 10 pm but no one had moved. Many officers had to know what was happening. They had come in full military gear as was the norm of the courtroom for any serving officer. The wives of the officers and the soldiers were anxious that the Colonel win the trial.

The fact that this officer had left everything to be with his beloved in her time of need played on their sentiments. Love and war had a strange kinship in the armed forces. They were sure it was his loving care which had helped them survive. Such emotions were generally seen in army camps during times of war. For a court martial, which very few can understand, such euphoria was incomparable.

Vikram, after greeting the presiding judge, started his submission.

"My Lord, I am grateful to you for giving me an opportunity to present my views before your honour. I have not risked my life for nothing – nor are these medals on my chest, a favour. I have earned it with my hard work, sincerity and dedication."

"As an officer, I stood for the right of a human being and the struggle to uplift humanity. A country means nothing if it doesn't care for core humans values and human beings. As a country, we respect it. That is why India is incredible. We, army men, stand for values and try to improve the lives of those who are suffering. We consider this motto as our core value and hold it close to our hearts."

"The truth is tough. It has always been. It is relative, too. One needs courage to listen to the truth. A country is made up of people whom we protect and, in this endeavour, even the life of one person matters. People make a country. I still believe in my actions. When she needed me, I stood by her, undaunted by the fear of death, like a true soldier. I am proud of my upbringing, ethos and fearlessness which I learnt in the army. I acted the way I had to, and I am not bothered about what fruits it will bear. I am alive now and may not be so after a while, but I stood with my head high in the face of enemy bullets and I stand high, bowing to the love of my life. I can tell my parents that I didn't stumble when my country needed me to embrace death nor when my beloved wanted me to take care of her during this unique disease."

"I would not have cared about the trial but for the reason that I stand for optimism, confidence and renewal of love, which the prosecution strangely finds superfluous. My emotions and sentiments cannot be expressed in legal language. It is prerogative of poets, painters and musicians to express the lover's narrative. Whatever I am arguing is a perfect logic of something unforeseen in the army. Let it be a myth that the army doesn't support love. I have not sinned nor do I apologise for what I did because it has given me new life. I intended to reclaim my love. For me, compassion is my primary duty. For me, having acted to uphold the biggest *dharma* of humanity, punishment would be an abuse of power. I am sure a judicious decision will be taken considering the factors. I am proud of my love, the way I am proud of the army and my country. I rest my argument. *Jai Hind*."

He sat feeling, satisfied. He could sense silent appreciation for his impassioned plea from those present in the courtroom.

The court adjourned for half-an-hour.

57

12.30 am, 2nd June, 2020
70th day of Lockdown

All eyes were on the Judge-Attorney. It was verdict time. Nisha had closed her eyes, bowed her head and was praying. Kohli was smiling, but was a mass of nerves, inside. His nervousness was visible in spite of his best efforts to hide it. Vikram was calm. The prosecution was worried. The arguments had taken on an emotional note, Vikram had appealed to the human sentiments of the bench to take a stand.

The presiding judge consulted the other judges for almost one hour and forty minutes. Their deliberated on balancing personal life with professional life, the growing demand of the young generation for wider personal choices in life and more freedom. You get only one life to live, so enjoy it to the hilt.

The unwritten code of the army is care – the forces care about their foot-soldiers, but at times they become adamant. The strict hierarchy and the old-world discipline do not allow them to discuss personal issues freely or become emotional in their speech and expression, though it fights wars by stirring the emotional cord. To what extent compassion and care should be part of its man-management profiling. What is war-time discipline and what is peace-time law of conduct? To what extent soldiers are guaranteed fundamental rights? It was not an easy discussion.

'Order, order.' The hammer commanding 'order' cut through the noise in the courtroom. A pin-drop silence descended on the small crowd that had gathered to hear the verdict.

"We are here to pronounce our judgment," Brigadier Patel said. He paused for a minute. The silence stretched like an eternity for everyone in the court. Not only for Nisha, Vikram and Kohli, the verdict could be a defining moment for the army, as well. Vikram was strangely nonchalant. Nisha clasped her hands in fervent prayers and Kohli appeared composed, at least on the outside.

The churn of emotions on the faces was myriad – one could feel the tension palpable in the air like a solid tangible thing.

The prosecution was playing for time – it was dispassionate and unruffled, waiting for the verdict.

In the army, court marshals were held to enforce discipline and not to decide against those breaking rules or laws.

Why should the court take a different stand this time? Vikram thoughts spanned from nonchalance to indignation – and then to cold white rage.

But he dared not show his emotional turbulence at this crucial moment. He had to think fast if the verdict went against him.

Brigadier Patel cleared his throat.

"The accused is honourably acquitted from the charges of act of cowardice, desertion from the army and conduct unbecoming of an officer. However, he is discharged from service for absenting without leave as a commanding officer. His pension, medals and honours, however, will remain protected."

Nisha broke into tears of joy. Kohli's eyes were misty, even though he was smiling in relief. Vikram closed his eyes and thanked god. History had been written. Love won the war, even in the army. The world would surely redefine the code of conduct for its warriors, at a time when the medical fraternity had proved to be a better warrior than all the other sentinels of the nation. He felt like a knight, who had just won a crusade.

At the opening tune of the national anthem, everyone stood up.